WHO CAN DENY LOVE?

The Marquis put his arm around her, kissing her passionately, possessively, until she turned her face away.

"I will not frighten you," he said, imploring, "but, my darling, you are not only divine and ethereal, but also human. Let me take you away —find a house—we will be alone!"

He kissed her once again and departed.

It was then she gave a cry that seemed to come from the very depths of her being. "I love him," she sobbed. "I love him. But . . . I am not a . . . I cannot do . . . what he asks!"

Bantam Books by Barbara Cartland
Ask your bookseller for the books you have missed

Barbara Cartland's Library of Love series

Other Books by Barbara Cartland

Who Can Deny Love?

Barbara Cartland

BANTAM BOOKS · LONDON
TORONTO · NEW YORK

WHO CAN DENY LOVE?
A Bantam Book / November 1979

ISBN 0–553–13330–6

Published simultaneously in the United States and Canada

Bantam Books are published by Bantam Books, Inc. Its trade-
mark, consisting of the words "Bantam Books" and the por-
trayal of a bantam, is Registered in U.S. Patent and Trademark
Office and in other countries. Marca Registrada. Bantam
Books, Inc., 666 Fifth Avenue, New York, New York 10019.

Author's Note

Works of Art have been forged for centuries—usually the imitation being for profit.

Albrecht Dürer was obliged to obtain an Imperial decree declaring the imitation of his woodcuts and engravings a criminal offence. The art of faking has flourished since the Rococo period, when petty Princes and newly created nobles employed the forgers because they wished to display famous works of Art.

Today the demands of American and Arab millionaires are so enormous that even the long-established centres of "faking," such as Paris, Rome, Florence, Vienna, and Madrid, find it almost impossible to keep up with the demand.

The most famous modern forgers were Hans van Meegeren, who admitted to painting the Vermeers which were "discovered" between 1935 and 1945, and the sculptor Alceo Dossena, who in 1927 voluntarily disclosed the secret of his forgeries.

Both these men produced such magnificent fakes that their work may be regarded as something much more significant than mere fraud.

He was quite certain that she had no

Who Can
Deny
Love?

Chapter One

1802

The Marquis of Fane drove his superfine horses down St. James's Street, conscious that his enemies and many of his friends were watching him with envious eyes.

It was not only because of his horses that the Marquis aroused envy, jealousy, and other violent emotions in people's hearts.

He was too good at everything to be anything but a controversial figure, and it was not surprising that he had a bad, positively raffish reputation even amongst those who circulated round the Prince of Wales.

As a sportsman the Marquis commanded the respect of the sporting-world, but he also infuriated those who competed against him in horse-raising, because he was so cock-sure of being the winner that they felt it was almost unfair that he should pass them at every winning-post.

In other types of sport, especially where it concerned the "fair sex," inevitably the Marquis captured the most beautiful women from under the noses of friend and foe alike.

He was reputed to have left more broken hearts behind him than any *Beau* in the last century.

1

His conquests at times annoyed even the Prince of Wales.

"I cannot understand what they see in you, Fane," he had remarked disagreeably only a week ago.

This was when he learnt that a dancer who had caught his eye on the stage at Covent Garden was already under the Marquis's protection.

His Royal Highness did not expect a reply to his question, because the answer was obvious.

The Marquis was not only extremely handsome but extraordinarily wealthy and possessed houses containing treasures that his family had accumulated since the reign of Elizabeth I.

That he was also self-sufficient, cynical, and declared openly that he had never been in love proved an irresistible challenge to women.

"There is no female born who does not wish to reform a rake," one of the older members at White's had said the previous evening, "but where Fane is concerned they might as well try to stop a forest-fire with a bucket of water!"

This remark was evoked by the news that Lady Isabel Chatley had left London owing, the newspapers said, to "an indisposition which obliged her to rest in the country air."

Everyone was well aware that neither the country nor any other sort of air was likely to cure the broken heart she had suffered at the hands of the Marquis of Fane.

He had grown bored with her when the Court returned to London at the beginning of April.

By the end of the month everyone knew of her feelings and his indifference, and had listened to her continual cry that she wished she were dead.

That she had given up the chase and retired to the country was a relief to those who were bored by her complaints. At the same time, they all agreed that the Marquis had as usual behaved badly.

He might have guessed before he started his

flirtation, if that was what it was, that Lady Isabel was the "clinging sort."

"It is no excuse that she is a damned good-looking woman!" another Club member said ruminatively. "All Fane's women are that. It is just that he is so insensitive to other people's feelings that he has no idea of the painful consequence of his interest, which never lasts long."

Those listening to the two old gentlemen found themselves wishing that their "interest" in women brought them even half the results that the Marquis achieved so easily.

It seemed to those who were sipping their brandy and considering how they should spend their evening that the Marquis had much more fun out of life than they did.

That was a thought that was galling to say the least of it.

The Marquis, with an expertise which was as remarkable as everything else he did, turned his horses at the end of St. James's Street towards Carlton House.

Actually he was thinking it was rather a bore that the Prince had sent for him when he had intended on returning to his house in Berkeley Square to change for his dinner-engagement with Lady Abbott.

She had commanded his attention last night at Devonshire House because the gown she wore was so transparent that when she entered the room he had, for one startled moment, thought that she was completely naked.

He must have met Lady Abbott on a number of previous occasions, but he had never before noticed that her figure was outstanding until the transparency of her gown had been brought so forcibly to his notice.

It was then that he decided she was worth more than a casual glance, and there was no doubt that the lady in question was only too willing.

Her dark hair and slanting green eyes reminded

him of a panther and he found when he talked with
her in the garden that she could flirt provocatively
and with the kind of sophistication that he always
found amusing.

Like the Prince, the Marquis preferred women
who were well versed in the art of love and the ways
of the world.

Although anxious mothers scuttled their offspring
away at his approach as if even by looking at him
they might become contaminated, young girls in fact
were perfectly safe from him. The Marquis was not
even aware of their existence.

When his relatives were brave enough occasionally to suggest to him that it was time he married
and had an heir, he set them down abruptly.

At the same time, he thought to himself that
if he did marry it would have to be a widow who
understood the Social World in which he moved and,
what was more important, understood his need to be
constantly amused and entertained.

There was nothing the Marquis dreaded more
than boredom, and he took care that he was seldom
in either the company or the situation where he might
conceivably be bored even for a few minutes.

When he was racing, boxing, watching a Mill, or
hunting, the activity stimulated him. Similarly, he
found himself amused when the pursuit of some attractive prey was difficult or prolonged.

The trouble where women were concerned was
that they fell far too easily into his arms almost before he held them out.

Although he looked forward to spending the evening with Lady Abbott, he had the uncomfortable
feeling that it would end predictably like every other
evening when he found a woman desirable and she
capitulated all too soon.

He drew up outside the fine Corinthian portico
added to Carlton House by Henry Holland.

The house was still far from finished but was already acclaimed as a triumphant success by those

who supported the Prince, and stigmatised as a costly failure by those who did not.

It was well known that the Prince's debts were rising towards half-a-million pounds, a great deal of which had been incurred in rebuilding and redecorating the sumptuous Palace, which, it had been averred, "had no spot without some finery upon it, gold upon gold."

Others said openly that it was vulgar in its opulence.

The Marquis appreciated that the Prince had outstandingly good taste, and although His Royal Highness spent a lot of money he did not possess, he was quite certain that posterity would believe it to be justified.

As he walked into the splendid Hall, decorated with Ionic columns of brown Siena marble, which led to an octagon and graceful double staircase, he thought, as he had thought before, that the Prince had an artistic sense for which the public never gave him credit.

Because the Prince had a Cosmopolitan mind and education, he had sent his friends and Agents to France, whenever the exigencies of the Revolution and the subsequent wars allowed it, to buy furniture and objets d'art.

They had brought back paintings, clocks, looking-glasses, bronzes, Sèvres china, and tapestries, and now at last they had a setting worthy of them.

As the Marquis walked up the stairs without hurrying, he knew that with the help of the Sales-Rooms and Dealers in London, the Prince had accumulated the most comprehensive collection of works of Art ever assembled by an Englishman, let alone by a future Monarch.

The Marquis had in fact helped to find and improve the collection with paintings by Pater, Greuze, Le Nain, and Claude, which the Prince had hung in his new rooms in a manner which commended itself to any Art-lover.

The extraordinary thing was that amongst the men with whom the Prince surrounded himself, many of whom were very intelligent, few had the same appreciation of Art as the Marquis had.

This was because in his own houses he had inherited paintings and treasures which compared very favourably with those that the Prince was accumulating.

He was also aware that the Queen had said angrily:

"The Marquis of Fane encourages George to spend money simply by flaunting his own possessions in front of him."

This was not quite true.

The Marquis could not help it if the Prince of Wales, whenever he stayed at Fane Park in Hertfordshire or visited Fane House in Berkeley Square, felt he must "go one better" than his friend.

The Prince was waiting for him in the Drawing-Room decorated in the Chinese style which many people of cultured taste in England had admired since the 1750s.

The Prince had become enamoured of it after he had seen the Temples and pagodas which Sir William Chambers, a leading architect at the time, had built at Kew for his grandmother.

He had actually sent an Agent to China to buy furniture for this room, for which it was said the bill amounted to £6,817, including £441 for lanterns alone.

This evening, however, the Prince was not interested in the decorations of this room, but in a painting standing on the floor propped against one of the sofas, which he had been contemplating when the Marquis was announced.

He looked up excitedly, saying:

"There you are, Virgo! And a devil of a time you have been getting here!"

"Forgive me, Sire," the Marquis apologised casually. "I was not at home when your message arrived, but immediately I returned I obeyed your request."

"Well, you are here and that is all that matters," the Prince said quickly. "Come and look at this!"

The Marquis moved across the room with an expression of slight annoyance on his face because he had, from the urgent wording of the Prince's note, expected something more interesting and dramatic than yet another painting.

He was flattered that his opinion was usually asked before the Prince bought anything in the Art World. At the same time, he was regretting that he had not waited to bathe and change first; then he could have gone straight from Carlton House to Lady Abbott.

The painting was a large one and, he noted, in extremely good condition.

Many of the Prince's purchases were black with age and dirty, and on being cleaned did not justify the excitement His Royal Highness felt about them.

This, however, was clearly a fine painting and after he had looked at it for one moment the Marquis said, drawling the words slowly:

"It appears to be a Van Dyck."

"That is what it purports to be," the Prince said. "Look more closely, Virgo. Do you not notice anything?"

A note of excitement in the Prince's voice made the Marquis concentrate on the painting more closely than he had done before.

He saw that the robes the Madonna was wearing of red and dark blue were very much in the Van Dyck style, and the exquisitely drawn hands bore unmistakably the artist's trade-mark.

The Holy Child, rosy and fat, was particularly brilliantly executed, and like many of his paintings showed a striking psychological insight.

Then he looked at the face of the Madonna and

there was suddenly an expression of surprise in his eyes.

The Prince, who was watching him, smiled delightedly.

"You notice it? I knew you would. It struck me the moment I saw the painting."

"It is certainly very similar," the Marquis murmured.

"There is no question about it," the Prince said. "Look for yourself."

He pulled from behind the sofa another painting, which had been hidden there, and turned it round to place it beside the Van Dyck.

It was a painting also of the Madonna, which he and the Marquis had thought to be an exceptional find the previous year.

Stephan Lochner's paintings were to be found on the Continent but none were known in England. However, the Prince had been able to buy one of his "fair and gentle" Madonnas, a delicate, dreamy figure, the contours of which seemed almost to melt into her surroundings.

It had been expensive because his paintings were so rare, and the Dealer who had bought it for the Prince had been able to tell him little of its history except that it had come from a private collecton.

The Prince had been in ecstasy over the painting, referring to it continually with a kind of lyricism.

But the Marquis had understood why the Lochner Madonna moved him so much, because he himself felt the same about it.

He was certainly not sentimental as the Prince was, and yet when he was looking at it, it evoked an emotion that made him feel that he was listening to a mediaeval love-ballad sung to the music of a spinet.

"Damn!" he had ejaculated later when he was alone. "I wish I had found that painting myself!"

He had in fact found it irresistible, and he seldom visited Carlton House, as he invariably did several times a week, without walking into the Music-Room to look at the painting, which they had discovered was called *The Virgin of the Lilies*.

This had been inscribed in small but elegant writing on the back of the frame, and while they thought it must have been added much later, the name had remained in the Marquis's mind.

Now, incredibly, so that he felt his eyes must be deceiving him, there was the same face portrayed by Van Dyck.

The composition was of course very different, and Van Dyck's painting was not so ethereal or so delicate, but there was no doubt that, seen side by side, the faces of the two Madonnas were identical.

The same large eyes, the same little straight nose, the perfectly curved lips, and the same rapt expression, almost one of ecstasy, as if some of the glory of Heaven was within her.

"It is extraordinary!" the Marquis exclaimed at length.

"That is exactly what I thought," the Prince remarked, "and yet how could it have happened, unless Van Dyck copied Lochner?"

"That is very unlikely," the Marquis replied. "From all we know about him, he was far too proud to think of copying another artist, and he always used models for his paintings."

"It would be impossible for him to use the same model as Lochner," the Prince said.

The Marquis nodded, knowing that when the Councillors of Cologne some seventy years after Lochner's death had proudly shown his *Adoration of the Kings* to Albrecht Dürer, a visiting celebrity, they could tell him nothing more about the artist except that he had come from Meersburg on Lake Constance and had died in the poor-house.

It had been generally accepted, however, that his death occurred sometime between 1451 and 1460.

As if he knew exactly what the Marquis was thinking, the Prince said:

"Van Dyck was born in 1599 and died in London in 1641."

"Then he must have copied the Lochner painting when he was abroad."

"I suppose so," the Prince said, "but it is very strange, since none of his other paintings portrays a face anything like this one, nor do they have such a delicate, spiritual quality."

"That is true," the Marquis agreed. "I suppose it is genuine?"

"Isaacs, who brought it to me, assured me that it is one of the best Van Dycks he has ever seen."

"Isaacs was selling it!" the Marquis remarked cynically.

He thought for a moment, then he said:

"It was Isaacs who brought you the Lochner."

"Yes, of course," the Prince replied. "I realised that."

"I am just wondering," the Marquis said, "whether in fact we are being deceived."

"If we are, then the painter is a genius in his own right," the Prince answered. "Look at the folds of that robe. Look at the texture of the child's skin. It is exactly in the Van Dyck tradition."

The Marquis, however, was looking at the Lochner, realising that there were other similarities besides the face, which a less experienced critic would not have noticed.

The robe in *The Virgin of the Lilies* was very different from that in Van Dyck's painting of the Madonna, and yet because he was so knowledgeable about Art, the Marquis thought there were certain brush-strokes that were identical in the two paintings, and something else too, to which he could not put a name.

He studied both works for a little while and knew that his instinct, which he had always trusted, told him there was something suspicious about both the paintings.

He knew the Prince was waiting for him to speak, and at last with a sigh he remarked:

"Strange, very strange—and for the moment I cannot find an explanation. I'll tell you what I will do, Sire. I will try to find out a little more about where Isaacs obtained these paintings."

"That is a good idea!"

"Have you bought much from him before?"

"Only the Lochner," the Prince replied. "He brought me two or three portraits which were not outstanding, so I did not even bother to show them to you. Then, as you know, we were both captivated by the Lochner."

His Royal Highness paused before he added:

"I paid more for it than I should have, but I still consider it was worth it."

"So do I," the Marquis agreed.

There was a faint smile on his lips as he remembered that while the Prince fixed the price, the Marquis paid the bill.

"Now let me think," the Prince said, putting his hand to his head. "Last year Isaacs brought me an El Greco which was too damaged to be interesting and a rather indifferent Van Dyck which I also refused."

"I remember that one. Anything else?"

"No, I think that is all, until he called today with this Van Dyck."

"It is certainly a very fine painting," the Marquis said. "But if you take my advice, Sire, you will say nothing about its resemblance to the Lochner until I have found out all I can about it."

"I will leave everything to you, Virgo," the Prince said. "You know I trust your judgement completely in anything that concerns Art."

The Marquis accepted this compliment as his right and did not dispute the Prince's good judgement. Instead he said:

"You have certainly aroused my interest, Sire, and I assure you I shall start work immediately in trying to discover where Isaacs obtained both these paintings. Now, I think we were somewhat remiss in allowing him to be so vague about the Lochner."

"You are right! Of course you are right!" the Prince agreed.

He gave an almost boyish smile as he said:

"I think we were both so delighted with it that we were eager to have it at any price without asking too many questions."

"It did cross my mind that it might be stolen," the Marquis said.

"And mine!" the Prince ejaculated.

"Now, if you will excuse me, Sire ..." The Marquis began, only to be interrupted as the Prince cried:

"You are not leaving, Virgo? If you are, come back and dine with me. I want to go on talking about paintings and a great many other things."

He was obviously disappointed. He often found it difficult to persuade the Marquis to be his guest although he enjoyed his company perhaps more than any of his other friends.

"There is nothing I would have liked more, Sire, had I known about it earlier, but you will understand that it would be extremely rude if I cancelled my dinner-engagement at the very last moment."

The Prince smiled.

"I can guess that you are dining with some 'fair charmer.'"

His eyes twinkled as he wagged his finger at the Marquis.

"Be careful, Virgo! You know as well as I do that your reputation is as bad as mine, if not worse, and we cannot afford to add to our list of crimes."

The Marquis smiled.

"Whatever we do or do not do, Sire, there will be people to talk about us, to exaggerate our every action, and, if that fails, to invent what they do not know."

The Marquis made an expressive gesture with his hands as he continued:

"Personally, if I have to be verbally hanged I prefer to have had the pleasure of committing the crime in question!"

The Prince threw back his head and laughed.

"That is good, Virgo, and very reassuring. I feel the same, so we will walk to the gallows together. Let us hope we will find that exercise worthwhile."

"I think that is likely, Sire," the Marquis replied, "and yet so often one is disillusioned."

"My dear Virgo," the Prince said, "you must not become a cynic."

"I am certainly not that where paintings and horses are concerned," the Marquis answered.

"Only with women?" the Prince questioned; then he added:

"Do not give up hope. Perhaps one day we shall find the 'Virgin of the Lilies' and she will be as lovely as Lochner portrayed her."

"I have a feeling that that would be impossible," the Marquis remarked. "At the same time, it does not cost anything to go on hoping."

Again the Prince laughed, and the Marquis made his farewells and walked down the stairs.

As he was driving up St. James's Street on his way home, he found himself quite unexpectedly regretting that he had not accepted the Prince's invitation to stay and dine at Carlton House.

The conversation would be amusing, as it always was, and the food and wine excellent, but that was not the reason.

It was because quite suddenly the slanting green eyes of Lady Abbott did not, in retrospect, seem so attractive as they had earlier in the day.

Intruding on his memory of Her Ladyship's face was the delicacy of the Madonna in *The Virgin of the Lilies*.

Her eyes, dreamy and wistful, looked out on the world as if they saw an enchantment that was part of herself and seemed to emanate from the grace of her figure, holding a bunch of lilies in her arms and surrounded by them.

Her hair was fair and drawn back beneath the conventional crown, not one of jewels but of flowers, and there were at the corners of the painting small angels with pointed wings peeping down at her.

It was a face which the Marquis could not erase from his mind, and there was an expression in her eyes which he had not only never seen in any other painting but certainly in no living woman.

'If only I had known her,' he found himself thinking.

Then as he turned his horses from Piccadilly into Berkeley Square he told himself that he was being ridiculous and becoming obsessed with a painting in a manner which he would have found laughable in any of his contemporaries.

Lady Abbott would doubtless be amusing, as he expected, and if she at least put up a few defences and a little opposition to his advances, the evening would not be wasted.

He hoped the inevitable conquest would not be too easy or too soon.

*   *   *

Cyrilla opened the shabby, unpainted door of the house and carried her basket in carefully, putting it down on the floor before she shut the door behind her.

Picking it up again, she walked along the narrow passage and into a small kitchen at the back.

A woman with grey hair who stood stirring a pot over the stove looked round to say:

"There's no sign of the Doctor."

"He promised he would come," Cyrilla said in an anxious little voice, "but I am afraid he suspects we have no money to pay him."

"I don't doubt it," Hannah replied. "You bought everything I asked you to?"

"Yes, Hannah, and it took our last penny. We

have nothing left unless Mr. Isaacs comes today with the money for the painting."

"He should have been here before now," Hannah said abruptly. "I don't trust that man, and that's a fact!"

"He is the only Dealer who has been kind since Papa has been so ill; but I was thinking, Hannah, that we shall either have to sell something soon or starve!"

"What can we sell, now that there's not a picture left in the place?" Hannah asked sharply.

Cyrilla said nothing. She only took off the cloak she wore, thinking, as she did so, that she felt curiously tired and knowing that it was due to lack of nourishing food.

Everything they could afford went to buy the medicines the Doctor had prescribed for her father, while she and Hannah lived on vegetables and an occasional egg, having no money left to buy anything else for themselves.

It was three days since she had taken the Van Dyck, the one that Frans Wyntack had been painting before he was taken ill, to Solomon Isaacs.

Frightened at her own daring, Cyrilla had finished off the last necessary brush-strokes, then aged the whole painting with a process that Frans Wyntack had made curiously his own.

When her mother had been ill and in need of medical attention, Frans had realised that his own paintings would not sell, and he had said bitterly and violently to Cyrilla:

"If they will not buy my paintings I will teach them a lesson they will never forget!"

"What do you mean by that, Papa?" Cyrilla had asked.

"I mean," Frans Wyntack had replied, "that when I was learning to be an artist, many years ago in Cologne, I found out how to paint fakes."

Cyrilla had stared at him wide-eyed, and he had gone on:

"There was a man I knew who was a bit mad.

He used to sit in the Gallery painting all day. Because I saw him so often, I began to take an interest in what he was painting."

"He was copying the paintings for sale at the Gallery?" Cyrilla asked.

"Yes," Frans Wyntack agreed, "but so skilfully, so cleverly, that sometimes he would laugh and hold up the painting and say:

" 'Now, if you saw that framed, would you know which was the original?' "

"They were as good as that?"

She had not really believed what Frans Wyntack had said to her, because she knew that he himself was very scornful of fakes and the Dealers who "touched up" paintings to make them more saleable.

"What happened to him, Papa?" she had asked.

He had stopped talking and his thoughts were obviously far away in the past.

"The artist?" he asked. "Oh, he occasionally sold one of his paintings to somebody who wanted a really good copy. But I expect he died of starvation, like so many of our kind."

"But I do not understand . . . why are you telling me . . . about it . . . now?" Cyrilla asked.

"I am telling you because before I left Cologne he taught me the secret of painting a picture in exactly the same style as the original famous artist's. It meant treating the canvass, using certain kinds of paint, and, when the work was actually finished, giving it a polish which would make it impossible for any purchaser to know that it had not been painted centuries earlier."

Cyrilla looked at him wide-eyed as he went on:

"That is what I intend to do now, and because of the way I have been treated by the Art World, shall put the money in my purse without having any guilty conscience about it!"

"But . . . Papa . . . that will be . . . cheating! Besides . . . forgery is a . . . punishable offence!"

"Only if you are caught," Frans Wyntack replied.

Although she had tried to argue with him, he had gone off to Sir George Beaumont swearing that he would paint a picture which would be so like the original that nobody would know the difference.

Cyrilla was aware that Sir George Beaumont, who had once come to the house to see her father, was a noted Patron of the Arts.

Because in England there were no public Picture-Galleries as there were abroad, Sir George would allow artists to examine his own collection and even copy the famous paintings he possessed.

Frans Wyntack used to make sketches and notes of a painting he liked and then paint a copy of it at home. He would then sell it to a Dealer and go back to Sir George's house to choose another.

When the paintings were completed, Cyrilla was absolutely astounded by them.

"They are brilliant, Papa! Actually brilliant! But I am sure it is wrong."

She could not, however, help feeling excited, if rather guilty, when a week later Frans Wyntack gave her enough money not only to pay the bills they owed but also to buy everything they needed for her mother for at least a week or so.

"I have to find another Dealer, and that is a difficulty," Frans Wyntack had confided.

"What is wrong with the one who has always handled your paintings?" Cyrilla suggested.

"It is far too dangerous to keep going to him. He knows me. He has been here and he knows quite well that I do not own anything of value."

"Then why has he bought the paintings from you?"

Her father laughed.

"He thinks I have stolen them—therefore, he is not prepared to ask questions."

"Oh ... Papa ... how could you let ... anyone think you are a ... thief?"

"I am prepared to let him think I am a great many other things as long as he pays me enough,"

Frans Wyntack replied. "Unfortunately, however, crime did not pay in this instance. I was beaten down to a lower figure than I had intended to accept."

He spoke angrily, and Cyrilla said:

"At least it has bought everything we need for Mama and has paid the Doctor's bill."

"He has been here today?" Frans Wyntack asked quickly.

Cyrilla nodded.

"What did he say?"

"That she needs rest and good food. He gave me a list of more medicines for her. None of these we have tried so far is any good."

Frans Wyntack's lips tightened, and when he left Cyrilla she heard him hurrying up the stairs to her mother's room.

Cyrilla stood listening until she heard the bedroom door close, then she said to herself:

"Mama must never know what Papa is doing. She would be shocked ... horrified at the idea of his painting fakes deliberately to defraud those who buy them. It is wrong ... very wrong ... but I do not see what else he can do."

Whatever they bought, her mother grew worse.

Every day she seemed thinner and weaker and the only time her eyes lit up and she seemed happy was when Frans Wyntack came into the room.

Then the colour would come into her face and for a few moments she would look as young and lovely as her daughter.

But nothing anyone could do could save her. She seemed to slip away from them, and one morning when Frans Wyntack awoke he found her dead beside him.

To Cyrilla it was as if the whole world had collapsed. Her life, her happiness, everything that meant home to her had been centred round her mother.

Without her she felt as if she drifted like a boat without a rudder, at the mercy of the waves and with no idea how to steer herself or in what direction to go.

If she was almost prostrate with grief, so was Frans Wyntack.

Day after day he sat in his Studio, staring at a canvass on which he occasionally painted small pictures of her mother's face and head, then rubbed them out as he felt they were not good enough to portray the woman he had loved.

"You'll have to get him painting again," Hannah said firmly. "There's no money, and even if you're not hungry, Miss Cyrilla, I certainly am!"

Cyrilla realised that Hannah was talking common sense.

Quietly but determinedly, she told Frans Wyntack that he had to paint, for there was nothing else they could sell.

At first he rebelled against continuing with the fakes he had sold for her mother's sake and went back to painting his own pictures.

But these fetched only a few shillings each. Usually, in fact, the price barely paid for the canvasses on which they were painted, and they would stand dusty and unnoticed in some Art-Dealer's shop.

Sadly Cyrilla sold the few things of any value that her mother had possessed—a painted shawl, a lace scarf, a fur muff—and when they were gone, she went to the Studio and said:

"One of us will have to earn money. Perhaps I could get a job scrubbing floors. I am not talented enough to do anything else."

Frans Wyntack looked at her as if he were seeing her for the first time.

She had been very like her mother when he had first seen her, and he had thought she was the most beautiful creature he had ever imagined in his wildest dreams.

Unhappiness and hunger had now sharpened Cyrilla's face until her little chin seemed very pointed and her eyes very large.

She was speaking to him early in the morning, before they had eaten breakfast, so she had not yet arranged her hair and it fell over her shoulders in a shining cloud the very pale golden colour of dawn.

Strangely enough, her hair had a touch of silver in it, as if a little of the moonlight had been left behind by mistake.

He stared at her in a way that made Cyrilla wonder what he was thinking. Then he said:

"I started a painting—a fake of a Lochner—when your mother was ill, but I couldn't finish it! God knows if I can ever capture the spirit of it, but I will try."

"What are you talking about, Papa?"

"You want money, so you have to earn it," he said almost harshly. "Drape that silk about you and sit on the throne over there."

"You are making me your ... model?" Cyrilla asked unnecessarily.

Frans Wyntack did not even bother to reply. He was setting up his easel, finding the unfinished canvass he wanted, and arranging her so that the light from the window was on her hair. Then he started to work.

The ethereal Madonnas for which Stephan Lochner was famous had reminded him of his wife. So he had wanted to paint this one almost as a portrait of her, not only because it would be very saleable but because he was never content with anything less than perfection.

He painted three other pictures while he was still working on the one for which Cyrilla was now the model.

The three, which he described as "pot-boilers," he copied as before from paintings in Sir George Beaumont's collection, and sold them to the same man who thought he had stolen them. This brought in enough money to keep Hannah from grumbling.

He went on working on the copy of the Lochner painting for months.

Finally, when he had finished, he made Cyrilla stand beside it, and said:

"Now look! Criticise! Use your instinct. Is there anything wrong?"

"It is absolutely beautiful, Papa! I wish I really looked like that."

"You do look like that," he said positively. "However, I am concerned not with your looks but with my painting."

"It is brilliant! You know it is brilliant! But why can you not make a painting like that yourself instead of a copy, and sign it with your own name and become famous?"

There was silence for a moment, then Frans Wyntack said:

"Shall I tell you the truth? Because I do know the answer."

"Tell me."

"Artists like Lochner and all those others whom you and I admire had a certain genius within them, something that made them paint as other men, however artistic they may think they are, are unable to do."

"I think what you are saying, Papa, is that they are like musicians who may be very musical but who cannot compose."

"Exactly! A composer is a genius. A painter has to have the same genius in him. If it is not there, the painting does not 'come to life,' and that is what is wrong with mine."

"But, Papa, you are so clever. This painting is beautiful! I would like to keep it and look at it every day."

Frans Wyntack laughed.

"You have only to look in the mirror, my dear. But this painting is going to bring us a lot of money."

"How?" Cyrilla enquired.

"I am going to a new Dealer, a man named Solomon Isaacs. I have heard he is eager for paintings which he can show to the Prince of Wales."

"You will not tell him it is a fake?"

"No, of course not! I am going to say that it is a painting I inherited, which has been in my family for years and with which I have not had to part until now."

He smiled as if he mocked at himself, then said to Cyrilla:

"Find me my best clothes, the ones in which your mother always said I looked like a gentleman. I hope they have not all been eaten away by the moths."

"No, of course not, Papa," Cyrilla replied indignantly. "Hannah will have seen to that."

Dressed as a gentleman, although a slightly old-fashioned one, Frans Wyntack had left the house with the "Lochner" painting, while Cyrilla, even though she thought it reprehensible, prayed that he might be successful.

Hannah was being very disagreeable about having no money to spend on food; and because Cyrilla felt that it was more important that her father should eat than that she and Hannah should, she often felt uncomfortably empty inside and weak in a manner which she knew quite well was due to lack of nourishment.

When she heard her father's knock at the door, for a moment it had been impossible to rise to her feet and go to open it.

She was so afraid, terribly afraid, that he had been disappointed and she would find him standing outside with the painting still under his arm.

Instead, he walked into the house with a cry of delight, picked her up in his arms, and swung her round in the same way that he had when she was a child.

"We have won! We have won!" he cried.

"You have sold the painting?" Cyrilla asked, breathless and a little dizzy.

"I have sold it, provided the Prince buys it, which the Agent is quite certain he will do. He wants a Lochner in his collection, and Isaacs is considerably impressed!"

"I want money now!" Hannah said sharply from the kitchen-door.

"Well, you will have to wait for it, woman," Frans Wyntack replied, "or get things on credit."

"You know I can't do that," Hannah retorted. "If your picture's not paid for in the next twenty-four hours, we'll all be in our graves, you mark my words!"

She went back into the kitchen and slammed the door.

Cyrilla and her father looked at each other in consternation, then laughed quietly almost like two conspirators.

"It is all right," he said. "As a matter of fact, Isaacs was so impressed with the Lochner that he gave me a few pounds on account."

"Oh, Papa! Why did you not say so?" Cyrilla asked. "You have upset Hannah quite unnecessarily."

"I was going to buy some food as a surprise," Frans Wyntack replied, "but then I could not resist coming home first to tell you what had happened."

Cyrilla smiled.

It was so like him to behave in such an irrational manner. In a way, she could understand that it was because he lived in a fantasy-world, and that was what had made her mother love him.

She had loved him so that she had been content to make sacrifices that no other woman would have made.

But Cyrilla swept the thought from her mind and said practically:

"Give the money to me, Papa. I will go and buy the food. You will buy all the wrong things, and I know exactly what Hannah wants."

Frans Wyntack was quite content to allow her to do as she suggested.

While she slipped away to the local shops that were only round the corner from the mean street in which they lived, he went to his Studio to start painting what he deluded himself into believing would be his masterpiece.

Chapter Two

"Really, M'Lord, there's nothing more I can tell you," Solomon Isaacs said, throwing out his hands in an expressive gesture.

The Marquis, very large and awe-inspiring in the untidy shop, looked at him searchingly.

"You told me," he said slowly, "that the owner of the Van Dyck wishes to remain anonymous, and that I can understand. At the same time, you realise I cannot advise His Royal Highness to buy a painting that has no dependable history behind it."

He paused to add impressively:

"It might be stolen, or even proven to be fake."

The Dealer gave an exclamation that was almost a scream of protest.

"I've my reputation to preserve, M'Lord, and I can assure you that after years of selling fine paintings to real connoisseurs, I can smell a fake a mile off."

The Marquis was not particularly impressed by his protest.

He knew that Isaacs, while he had a good reputation in the trade, was not one of the most important Dealers in London.

At the same time, he was aware that the Jew was noted as being sharp, intelligent, and genuinely knowledgeable where paintings were concerned.

"Have you had any other paintings from this particular source?" he enquired.

There was just a faint pause before Solomon Isaacs replied:

"No, M'Lord, this is the first one."

He said it quite convincingly, but the Marquis knew he was lying.

Playing for time, he looked round the shop, which was in a side-street turning off Bond Street.

There were a number of paintings hung on the walls which were of no interest to the Marquis and which he knew would not evoke a second glance from the Prince of Wales.

There were also a number of canvasses on the floor, stacked against the walls, and also a collection of frames.

He walked over to the nearest pile of canvasses.

"Show me these," he ordered.

Isaacs hurried to obey, turning them round into the light which came from the door and a window which needed cleaning.

He then burst into the usual patter of an Art-Dealer:

"The colour of this one is outstanding—look at the texture—the brush-strokes—the light in the eyes of the model."

The Marquis had heard it all far too often even to listen to what was being said. He merely decided that the majority of the paintings were rubbish or of subjects which he had never liked and would not have purchased however well they were painted.

The first stack of canvasses was exhausted and he turned to another.

The same thing happened, Isaacs sometimes holding a painting for so long while he eulogised that the Marquis had to make a gesture of refusal before he produced another.

Finally, when even the Dealer's volubility came to a standstill, the Marquis said:

"Now we come back to my original question. What more do you know about the Van Dyck?"

"What can I say?" Solomon Isaacs asked, with almost a note of desperation. "I've told Your Lordship everything that I myself know about it."

"Then find out more. His Royal Highness will not accept the painting until he is better informed."

The Marquis spoke sharply and walked towards the door.

Then, as he expected, Isaacs was by his side, pleading with him.

"I'll do all I can, M'Lord, but I can't do the impossible. I'll try, that I promise you, I'll try!"

"Do not be too long about it," the Marquis said.

He would have left, but once again Isaacs' voice prevented him.

"There's just one thing, My Lord, but I don't like to mention it."

"What is that?"

"The seller is desperate to be paid. She did indeed ask me—"

"She?"

The Marquis's ejaculation was like a pistol-shot.

As he spoke, he saw by the expression on the Jew's face that he knew he had made a slip of the tongue.

There was silence for a moment.

"You said 'she'!" the Marquis remarked slowly. "Are you telling me this painting belongs to a lady?"

"The lady called here yesterday," Solomon Isaacs conceded. "She said that her father, who owns the painting, is very ill and they need the money so that he can have proper medical attention."

The Marquis had the feeling that the words were being dragged out of the man, but he was not aware that Isaacs was embarrassed because he not only had no wish to reveal the source from which he had obtained the painting but he also felt that the Marquis would not be impressed by the lady's address.

She was poorly dressed and arrived on foot, and alone, which told Isaacs before she spoke that she was not exaggerating when she said she needed the money.

It struck him, because he was a sharp salesman, that the lady could be forced into accepting less for the painting than she had asked and he could make a larger profit.

He had the uncomfortable feeling that the Marquis, for whom he had the highest respect as a business-man, might be able to circumvent this if he actually found out from where the painting had come.

In fact, his fears materialised a moment later when the Marquis said:

"I think, Isaacs, I would like to meet this lady and discuss the painting she is selling. She should certainly be able to tell me more about it than you have been able to do."

"I think that'd be impossible, M'Lord," Isaacs said quickly—too quickly for the Marquis to be deceived.

"Why?" he enquired, though he was sure of the answer.

"I don't know her address, M'Lord."

"Then how do you intend to pay her?"

"She said she'd call here tomorrow."

"At what time?"

"She didn't say, M'Lord."

The Marquis thought for a moment.

"Do you think if you ask her for her address she will give it to you?" he questioned at length.

"I doubt it, M'Lord. I had the feeling that it was as the gentleman said, the one who brought the other painting to me—"

"What other painting?"

Isaacs was getting confused.

He knew it was not something he usually did, but the Marquis overwhelmed him, and he was also over-anxious to make the sale, which was always a mistake.

Everybody in the trade knew quite well that if they were to obtain their money, the Prince of Wales's purchases were usually paid for by one of his friends.

In the case of paintings, the Marquis of Fane had obliged His Royal Highness on a great number of occasions, and the money Isaacs had obtained for the Lochner had been delivered by a groom in the Marquis's livery and the bill-of-hand had been inscribed with his name.

"I think you told me a little while ago," the Marquis said slowly, "that this was the first painting you had from that particular source."

"I was mistaken," Solomon Isaacs admitted. "I remember now that the gentleman who brought me a painting which Your Lordship liked, and which His Royal Highness purchased, gave me the same address as this lady. It did not strike me before."

The Marquis was well aware that this was a lie, but he let it pass.

"What was his name?"

"That, I've given my word, M'Lord, not to reveal, and it'd be very unethical of me to do so."

"Then what was his address?"

"I have my principles, M'Lord. I wouldn't have my good name impaired. As I've said often enough —my word is my bond."

The Marquis looked annoyed and said:

"Your story becomes more twisted every second. The picture by Stephan Lochner which you sold to His Royal Highness six months ago came, you said at the time, from a private collection and you therefore knew very little about it."

"That's right, M'Lord."

"Now this painting, about which you have been extremely mysterious, apparently comes from the same source."

"I got muddled, M'Lord, because in this instance I've been dealing with a young lady and before that with a gentleman."

"She said it was her father."

"Yes, yes, M'Lord. She did say that."

"And he is ill?"

"Yes, M'Lord."

"So she is desperate for money."

"She is, M'Lord."

There was a glitter of triumph in the Marquis's eyes, although Isaacs did not notice it.

He was feeling, uncomfortably, that he had made a fool of himself.

The Marquis, as Isaacs had thought before, was very difficult to deal with.

"I have a suggestion to make to you," the Marquis said slowly. "I will buy this painting at the price you are asking, which I am as aware as you are is a somewhat inflated figure, only on one condition—that you give me the address at which the money is to be paid. There will be no need to give me the name, so you will not break your word, which apparently means so much to you."

There was a touch of sarcasm in the Marquis's voice which Isaacs did not like.

The Dealer hesitated because he was afraid not of offending the seller of the painting but of what the Marquis might discover.

The man who had sold him the Lochner had looked a gentleman although he was dressed in a somewhat old-fashioned manner and was obviously of foreign origin. But he had come to collect the money and only after he had been paid had it struck Isaacs that perhaps it might have been to his advantage to find out if he had any other paintings for sale.

After all, to please the Prince of Wales was the ambition of every Dealer in the whole country.

Isaacs had, although he had not shown it, been overjoyed when the young woman had brought him the Van Dyck.

Because she had looked poor and unimportant he had not at first paid any attention to her when she came into the shop a little hesitatingly carrying a canvass.

He was quite certain that she had nothing of importance to offer him, and he always found it good tactics to keep those who wished to approach him waiting to make a sale until they felt nervous and more anxious than they were already.

When finally he had asked the woman somewhat aggressively what she wanted, he had been surprised at the quiet, melodious quality of her voice.

He had been even more surprised, and very agreeably so, when he saw what she had brought him.

Otherwise he had not noticed her particularly. Since it was a cold, blustery day, she was wearing a long cape made of expensive material but which was shabby and unfashionable. It had a hood which she had pulled forward over her face.

Now, thinking of her, he found it difficult to remember exactly what she looked like.

At the time, he had had eyes only for the painting itself.

He had seen at a glance that it was not only a Van Dyck but a particularly fine example of the artist's work.

There was no mistaking the skilfully painted folds of the Madonna's robe, which reminded him of one that he had seen two years before, when he had made an exhausting but rewarding visit to Munich.

Of course, he was well aware that Van Dyck had painted hundreds of pictures including portraits and a series of magnificent Biblical scenes.

Charles I had settled an annual pension of two hundred pounds on him and presented him with two houses besides giving him a Knighthood.

Isaacs admired Van Dyck perhaps more than any other great artist and he had always longed to have one to sell.

This was the answer to one of his greatest ambitions and he could hardly believe his good luck as he stared at the painting which the woman in the cloak had brought to him.

"Where did you get this?" he managed to ask at last.

"It . . . it belongs to my father. He sold you a painting a little . . . while ago."

"Which one?"

"It was by . . . Stephan Lochner."

The woman seemed to stumble a little over the words, but Isaacs had almost given a shout of delight.

The Lochner with which the Prince of Wales had been so pleased, for which the Marquis of Fane had paid without haggling over the price, had been a tremendous coup.

Now he had another masterpiece from the same source, and he told himself that the Prince could not fail to be delighted with this really brilliant example of Van Dyck's work.

However, he thought it a mistake to show the seller how elated he was.

He managed to remark almost casually:

"I suppose you have your father's authorisation to sell this painting?"

"Yes . . . of course."

There was a little tremor in her voice and Isaacs did not understand that Cyrilla was feeling humiliated because she was certain that he thought she must have stolen it.

"In which case I'll take it from you and hope to find a buyer in a reasonable period of time."

"You . . you would not . . . buy it . . . outright?"

He shook his head.

"I seldom do that. What are you asking for it?"

He thought she might have no idea of its worth, but instead she mentioned, again hesitatingly, a figure which he knew was fair, though for a Van Dyck it was rather below the market-value.

"I doubt if I'll get that."

"Will you please try? It is very . . . important that my father should have the money as . . . soon as possible."

'Gambling-debts, I'll be bound!' Isaacs thought to himself.

And that, he imagined, would explain why the other painting had had to be sold.

They were always the same, these gentlemen, chucking away their money on the green baize tables, and when they had a bad run their families were left with hardly a crust to eat.

"I'll see what I can do," he said, "but it never pays to be in a hurry."

Cyrilla had drawn in her breath. Then she said, feeling ashamed because she must humble herself:

"Would it be ... possible for you to give me ... a little ... just a little ... on account? My father needs ... medicines and the Doctor has ... to be paid."

For a moment Isaacs was inclined almost automatically to refuse. Then some compassion which he did not know he possessed was aroused by the slim figure standing beside him.

Perhaps because the musical quality of her voice touched him in a way he had not expected, he put his hand into his pocket.

"I don't know why I should break my rules to please you," he said, excusing his generosity, "but here is five pounds. I shall of course deduct it and my commission from what I obtain for the painting."

As he spoke, he put five golden sovereigns into Cyrilla's gloved hand.

"Thank you... very much," she said. "It is ... very kind of you. I'll call in two days' time ... that will be Wednesday ... to see if by then you've managed to sell the painting."

"You must suppose I'm a magician if you think I can dispose of it as quickly as that! But come if you wish, and I would like to have your address. If you have anything else of the same sort to sell, you might as well bring it with you, or I will collect it."

He spoke with an effort to disguise his own eagerness.

A Lochner—and now this!

He was certain that the Prince of Wales would find the Van Dyck irresistible.

He had been thinking about what had happened for so long that he had almost forgotten the Marquis was waiting.

Now, to his consternation, he realised that the nobleman was walking out the door of the shop.

"M'Lord! M'Lord!" he cried.

"If you are not interested in my proposition," the Marquis said, "I quite understand. I will tell somebody in the Prince's household to return the painting to you."

"No, M'Lord! No, please, listen to me!" Isaacs pleaded.

The Marquis stopped on the pavement.

His Phaeton was waiting for him, with the two spirited horses which drew it fidgeting to be off.

"Well?" he asked in an uncompromising tone.

"It is—Seventeen, Queen Anne Terrace, Islington, M'Lord!"

As the Marquis began to climb into his Phaeton he said:

"You shall have the money for the Van Dyck in the morning."

The groom released the horses' heads and ran to jump up behind the high vehicle, the Marquis drove off, and Isaacs with a deep sigh went back into his shop.

He had the uncomfortable feeling that he had made a mistake, but what alternative had there been?

Queen Anne Terrace, in the poor part of Islington, was not the type of address where one would expect to pick up a masterpiece of the type of the Lochner or the Van Dyck.

He was more and more convinced that there was something peculiar about the paintings that he should have investigated before he offered them to the Prince of Wales.

He had felt that the gentleman who said he owned the Lochner was genuine, but the woman seemed different.

No lady of any pretention would have come to Bond Street alone. No lady would have carried a painting in her own hands.

He thought, as she left the shop after he had with some difficulty extracted her address, that the painting might have been stolen from someone in the country and the Police would have been notified of the theft.

A wiser and perhaps richer Dealer would have made enquiries, but Isaacs was in a hurry not only to be paid but also to please the Prince of Wales.

The first picture he had sold him had been a real feather in his cap, but one sale was not enough, although it had at least given him the *entrée* to Carlton House.

Only as the Phaeton disappeared did Isaacs say to himself:

"I should have given His Lordship a false address and he would then have been obliged to come back to me."

It struck him that the Marquis would have known he was lying just as he had known he lied when he had said he had no idea who the seller was.

It was infuriating to have been outwitted and outmanoeuvred.

"His Lordship's too clever by half, and that's the truth," he muttered to himself, not realising that people of a very different class from his own had said the same words, or something like them, over and over again ever since the Marquis had grown to manhood.

The Marquis was in fact at the moment delighted.

He had extracted the information he wanted and he knew now he could not wait but must start out on the chase, which he was already finding extremely intriguing.

Because life held few mysteries for him and practically no secrets, the Marquis was as alert as a hound following the scent of a fox, and he pushed his horses a little faster than usual through the crowded traffic which he encountered on his way to Islington.

This part of London had been fashionable in the middle of the last century but now had fallen on ill times.

The houses were badly in need of paint, their elegant wrought-iron balconies draped with washing, and many of the fan-lights over the doors were broken and stuffed with rags.

Queen Anne Terrace, however, was comprised of houses of various shapes, sizes, and periods, and it took the Marquis little time to find that number 17 was a house at the end, which had built onto it a strange erection which he realised might be an artist's Studio.

As his groom ran to the heads of the horses, he threw down the reins, stepped down to the pavement and walked up to the door, which was sadly in need of paint, and raised the brass knocker, which he saw to his surprise was well polished.

There was no response and he thought that perhaps his journey had been in vain and he would not be able to solve his puzzle as easily as he had expected.

Then as he raised the knocker again the door was opened and a voice said:

"Have you forgotten your key, Hannah?"

Then there was silence.

Cyrilla was staring at the Marquis in surprise, having expected to see Hannah on the doorstep.

He was looking at her with an astonishment which for a moment made him speechless.

Cyrilla's fair hair was silhouetted against the light at the end of the passage, which came from the open door of the kitchen, and it gave her a kind of halo, while the dark walls framed her and made her appear as ethereal and dream-like as Lochner's Madonna.

It might have been the passing of several seconds or several hours that they stood looking at each other. Then Cyrilla recovered her voice first.

"I . . . I am sorry," she said. "I thought you were my maid, who has gone shopping . . . and I think you must have . . . come to the wrong house."

Her voice, the Marquis thought, was exactly what he would have expected the Madonna in *The Virgin of the Lilies* to possess, and he replied, thinking even to himself that he sounded almost incoherent:

"Not at all—I meant to come here—to find you."

"To . . . find me?"

There was no doubt that Cyrilla did not understand what he was saying—which was not surprising.

The Marquis swept his tall hat from his head.

"May I come in?" he asked. "I have to talk to you."

Cyrilla's eyes widened, then with a hesitating, almost involuntary gesture she glanced over her shoulder as if for protection.

"I assure you I will not be any trouble to you," the Marquis said with a faint smile on his lips, "and I will leave the moment you wish me to do so. But it would be difficult to talk standing here in the doorway."

As he spoke, Cyrilla was aware that two people passing by were staring at the Marquis, doubtless surprised that anyone so obviously opulent should be in such a neighbourhood.

"Yes . . . of course," she said, with just a little tremor in her voice. "Please . . . come in. I am afraid my father is . . . ill and cannot . . . receive you."

As she spoke, she wondered swiftly what could be the reason for this gentleman's visit, and she asked herself if by some wonderful chance he had seen one of her father's paintings and wished to purchase it.

It was something she had often conjured up in her imagination and it would be too wonderful if it actually came true.

Her father had been painting for years and his works were on sale at quite a number of shops, not like the grand one to which she had taken the Van Dyck, but the smaller Art-shops that abounded in Islington.

She knew that those in search of an artistic bargain often visited these shops in the hope of finding an artist who would become fashionable overnight and thereby make their purchase worth a great deal more than they had paid for it.

The Marquis entered the small passage, seeming with his broad shoulders and elegance to make it shrink down even narrower than it was already.

Cyrilla opened a door on the left-hand side and he found himself entering the Sitting-Room.

It was a small room, but he recognised immediately that it was furnished in good taste even though there was nothing of any great value in it.

The skilfully made curtains, while of cheap material, blended with the walls and matched the cushions on the small sofa and two elegant chairs.

Almost instinctively the Marquis looked for paintings and saw that where they had hung there were only marks on the wallpaper which were less faded than the rest.

Then as his eyes were held by the girl facing him, he felt that he must be dreaming, for he was actually seeing what he had thought to be impossible —the model for *The Virgin of the Lilies*.

She was so beautiful that he could hardly credit that she was not a figment of the dreams he had dreamt about her.

Her features were delicate and her eyes so large and expressive that he knew he had been right in thinking that she personified a mediaeval love-ballad played to the music of a spinet.

'She is lovely, unbelievably lovely!' he thought to himself.

Then he realised he was staring and because of it a faint colour had come into her cheeks.

"Will you . . . sit down, Sir?" she asked, indicating one of the arm-chairs.

The Marquis did as she requested and Cyrilla sat opposite him.

She wore a very simple muslin gown without ribbons or any trimming, but because it was so simple, and yet revealed the soft curves of her figure, there was somehow an exact rightness about it.

She might, the Marquis thought, have been the Virgin Herself, very young, innocent, and untouched by the world, before the angel came to Her.

The Marquis thought he had never seen such expressive eyes or ones that had a spiritual beauty which was hard to describe even to himself.

Then, realising that Cyrilla was waiting for him to speak, he said:

"I am the Marquis of Fane. I am here because I understand you are the owner of a painting reputed to be a Van Dyck."

He thought she might be surprised, but he had not expected that the colour would seep over her face in a manner which made him think of the dawn sun rising on the horizon.

There was at the same time a stricken expression in her eyes, which made him feel he had been cruel to a child or to a small defenceless animal.

Her lips moved but no sound came from them, and after a moment, in what his friends would have found a surprisingly gentle voice, he said:

"I learnt your address from a man called Isaacs, who took the painting you wish to sell to His Royal Highness, the Prince of Wales."

Cyrilla clasped her fingers together and as she did so, the Marquis noted that her hands were exquisite, the sort of hands Van Dyck liked to portray.

"You should not be surprised to hear I immediately recognised the face in the Van Dyck as identical to that of the Madonna by Lochner, which Isaacs sold to the Prince some months ago," the Marquis remarked.

Now Cyrilla looked down in what he knew was embarrassment, and her eye-lashes were very dark against her cheeks, which had lost their colour and had become almost translucently pale.

"I am ... sorry," she said after a moment, her voice trembling.

"If you had not sat for both those paintings," the Marquis said, "I think I should have been as deceived by the Van Dyck as His Royal Highness and I were by the Lochner."

"It was ... stupid of me," Cyrilla murmured in a voice he could barely hear.

"Of you?" the Marquis asked. "Did you paint them?"

"No, no, of course not!" Cyrilla replied quickly. "It was ... Papa ... but please ... do not hurt him ... he is so very ... ill ... in fact I do not think he will ... live very long."

There was a little break in her voice which told the Marquis how distressed she was, and he replied quietly:

"Let me assure you I have not come here to make trouble, but to understand how two different artists, a hundred and fifty years apart, should have painted the same beautiful face and apparently used the same model."

He thought that Cyrilla seemed embarrassed by his compliment and he went on:

"Please explain. I am not being merely inquisitive; I should be fascinated to learn how it all happened."

Cyrilla's eyes were raised to his.

"You must be ... very shocked," she said. "I knew it was ... wrong ... very wrong ... but there was nothing ... absolutely nothing else ... Papa could do when Mama was so desperately ill ... and we had not enough money even to buy her food."

The Marquis did not speak and after a moment she repeated pleadingly:

"P-please ... understand ..."

There was something very moving in the desperate note in her voice, and the Marquis said:

"I want to understand, so could we start at the very beginning? Will you first tell me your name?"

"It is Cyrilla ... Wyntack."

"And your father is an artist?"

"Yes. His name is Frans Wyntack."

"He is not English?"

"No, he is half-Austrian and half-Flemish."

"That would of course account for his skill. I am not paying him a polite compliment, Miss Wyntack, when I say he paints so well that I cannot believe he would ever be short of money."

"That is what I have often thought," Cyrilla said, "but unfortunately no-one ... wants the pictures he ... paints."

The Marquis looked puzzled and she explained:

"I think perhaps he is in advance of his time. He believes light should be portrayed in a certain way on the object he has chosen, but those who buy paintings want everything to be ... conventional."

The Marquis was too well versed in Art not to understand what she was trying to say.

"I would like to see your father's paintings," he said, "but please explain to me why he painted these fakes and how he carried it off so brilliantly."

"It was something he did only ... because Mama was so ill. He learnt how to do it many years ago when he was in Cologne, and because we had no money he copied one or two paintings in Sir George Beaumont's collection, altering them enough to look as if they were other paintings by the Master he had chosen, and ... they sold."

"For large amounts?"

"No, for very ... little, because he took them to the ... shops round ... here."

"Then what happened?"

"Mama got worse," Cyrilla said in a low voice,

"and the ... Doctor said only special medicines might save her ... and Papa was so desperate ... that he started ... *The Virgin of the Lilies.*"

She paused. Then as the Marquis did not speak, she went on:

"He painted it while he was doing what he called 'pot-boilers.' He had memorised the background and the figure of the Madonna as he had copied a Lochner painting before, with the man who had taught him how to paint ... fakes when he was in ... Cologne. But he could not do the face without a model."

"So you sat for him," the Marquis said.

He saw the unhappiness in her eyes and knew that it had gone against every instinct in her body to be part of such a deception.

"It is one of the most beautiful paintings I have ever seen," he said aloud.

He saw the light come back into Cyrilla's eyes.

"I am so glad you think that. Because it was so ... beautiful, I somehow thought it ... excused the fact that Papa was ... pretending it was done by ... Stephan Lochner."

"I do not believe Lochner, or any other artist, could have done it better."

"Mama died before it was finished and he would not ... touch it for a long time. He ... went back to ... painting his ... own pictures."

"As I said before, I would like to see them," the Marquis said.

"I will show you one," Cyrilla replied.

She rose to her feet and the Marquis said:

"If you are going to your father's Studio, may I come with you?"

She looked a little startled at the request, then she said:

"If it ... pleases you, My Lord."

The Marquis opened the door for her and she walked ahead and up a short flight of stairs.

The Studio had been built out on the next floor.

It was large compared to the rest of the building, and there was a north window which was everything any artist could wish for.

There were the usual paraphernalia of easels, a model's throne, and canvasses smeared with paint or with a few lines of charcoal.

On one easel was a painting that Cyrilla had put there after taking away the Van Dyck on which Frans Wyntack had been working before he was taken ill.

It was as if subtly she was inviting him to paint as soon as he was well enough to leave his bedroom.

It was practically finished and there was in fact only a little of the background to be filled in.

The Marquis looked at it and understood exactly why it was unsaleable.

It had nothing about it that the average purchaser of works of Art would understand or appreciate. Yet he knew it had merit and that Wyntack was trying to express his feelings in a medium which no-one else had used.

For the model he had chosen a number of oranges lying on a table beside a vase of flowers.

He had painted them in great blobs of colour, picking up the light in brilliant patches that seemed at first glance to have nothing to do with the subject, and yet when one looked closer they intensified it.

As the Marquis stood looking at the painting, he was aware that Cyrilla was looking at him, hoping desperately that he would understand.

He sensed too that she was afraid he would laugh her father's efforts to scorn.

"I have a feeling," he said at length, "that your father is so far ahead of his time that, as you say, people do not understand what he is trying to portray. And yet I can quite honestly say that I consider this a very clever, if not brilliant, piece of work!"

She made a little sound of sheer joy. Then she said:

"I wish Papa could hear you. No-one has ever said anything like that to him. I think perhaps it would be worth all the disappointments, all the years in which he has felt he was a failure."

"It is the last thing I would say your father was," the Marquis replied, "but I suppose you are aware that all great artists, whether they are musicians, painters, or writers, have to fight to get a hearing, and usually only when an artist is dead is his work appreciated."

As he spoke he thought he had been rather tactless, seeing that Cyrilla knew that that was exactly what would happen to her father.

"I think," she said, "that to know that he would be understood and appreciated in time would make Papa . . . very happy. When he is well enough I will tell him what you have said."

"He is not well enough for me to speak to him now?" the Marquis asked.

Cyrilla shook her head.

"He has been . . . unconscious for the last three days. The Doctor came to see him this morning . . . and said there was . . . nothing he could do."

She spoke in a tight little voice that told the Marquis she was controlling her feelings.

"I would like to buy this painting," he said, "if you will allow me to do so."

He expected that she would be pleased, but instead she said quickly:

"No . . . of course . . . not."

He raised his eye-brows, and she explained, the colour rising in her cheeks:

"You are aware that Papa has tried to . . . deceive you with the Van Dyck? To make amends, perhaps I could give you the painting."

"You know that I could not accept such generosity in the circumstances," the Marquis said. "Let us be quite frank, Miss Wyntack—you need the money, and I would like to give it to you because I can see in this painting the merit which other people would miss."

She looked indecisive and he said with a faint smile:

"I think pride is something you should dispense with at the moment."

"It is not exactly ... pride," Cyrilla said, "it is because ... Mama would have been so ... shocked at Papa painting... f-fakes ... even though we were desperately in need of the money."

"I think your mother would have understood," the Marquis said. "And now, because I must discuss with the Prince of Wales what we should do about the Van Dyck, and because I know you must have the money immediately to spend, I am going to insist upon giving you fifteen pounds for this painting, which I intend to take with me now."

"It is too much!" Cyrilla cried.

The Marquis would have offered more, but he had a feeling that she would not accept it. He had therefore chosen a figure that he knew would seem quite considerable to her, while to him it was of no consequence whatsoever.

"I dislike arguments," he said, "and never enter into them if it is possible. So you must allow me to have my own way in this instance."

As he spoke, he drew some notes from the inner pocket of his driving-coat and put them down on the table.

Then he took the painting from the easel.

"I am going to show this to His Royal Highness," "It will be very interesting to see what his reaction is —whether it is the same as mine."

"Perhaps he will be very angry when he learns that the Lochner is a fake," Cyrilla said in a small voice. "Supposing he decides to prosecute Papa?"

"I will see that he does nothing of the sort," the Marquis answered. "You are not to worry, Miss Wyntack, and if you will allow me to do so, I will call on you tomorrow and see how your father is, and I hope, in all sincerity, that he will be much improved."

"So do I," Cyrilla said. "Thank you . . . thank you very much for being . . . so kind."

She looked up at him as she spoke, and the Marquis had an almost irresistible impulse to take her in his arms and see if she was real.

There was such a fairy-like quality about her, the feeling of beauty that Lochner had portrayed so brilliantly, but the Marquis still felt as if she were part of his imagination and had no substance in fact.

"How do you spend your days?" he asked.

She looked surprised at the question, then answered after a moment:

"My maid Hannah and I cannot leave the house at the same time. Someone always has to be looking after Papa."

"And when your father is well?"

"I still look after him," she said with a little smile. "He would never leave his Studio if I did not sometimes make him take me for a walk and, even though he hates it, accompany me to the shops, when we have any money to spend."

"It seems a strange life for anyone as lovely as you are."

He had spoken without thinking, and now he realised that he had startled her. Her eye-lashes were dark against her cheeks as she said quickly:

"I think I will hand this money over to Hannah. She will be glad . . . so very glad that I have sold a painting . . . so that we can buy the things Papa needs."

As she spoke, Cyrilla moved towards the door, but the Marquis deliberately walked to the big window of the Studio to look out.

Outside were the back-yards of Islington but he looked at them with unseeing eyes.

There were quite a lot of things he wanted to say but he had no idea how to put them into words.

He knew Cyrilla expected him to go, but he wanted to stay.

He felt strangely that if he left her he might never find her again, and yet now that he had discovered her, there should be no difficulty in the future.

He did not know quite what he was seeking, he only felt confused to the point where it was almost impossible to think clearly.

The Madonna in *The Virgin of the Lilies* was there, in her face, which he had looked at hundreds of times since the Prince of Wales had bought the painting; it was the face which had haunted his dreams and which he had thought belonged to a woman long since dead—but she was, unbelievably, alive! And her name was Cyrilla.

He knew without turning round that she was looking at his back and wondering why he did not go, and that she was in consequence a little uneasy.

And yet, was that true?

The Marquis knew in his heart that he had known Cyrilla since the beginning of time.

She had always been there in his mind and in his ideals.

Then he told himself that he was being ridiculously, absurdly sentimental, and if he spoke of this aloud she would think he was a madman and she would be quite right in doing so.

With an effort he turned from the window.

"I must leave you, Miss Wyntack," he said in a business-like tone, "but, as I have already said, I will return tomorrow. Is there anything I can bring you?"

It was almost an offhand question but it was one which invariably evoked the same response: the women he knew well would say: "Only yourself!" Others, with whom he was just beginning an acquaintance, would look coy and say: "I should be thrilled with anything you could give me!"

Cyrilla's answer was very different.

"You have been so kind . . . so generous," she said. "I only wish I could find the right words in which to thank you. Perhaps when Papa is better he can paint you something you would really like and we could give it to you in gratitude."

"I should appreciate that," the Marquis replied, "especially if it was a portrait of you."

She was still for a moment and he knew that a sudden thought had come to her.

"You have a portrait of yourself?" he asked.

"Not ... exactly," Cyrilla replied, "but one I would like to show you."

She went to a corner of the Studio and took from a drawer two small canvasses.

When they were in her hand she began to walk towards the Marquis, and he felt as if she floated rather than walked and he almost expected to see a white cloud beneath her feet.

When she reached him she held up the canvasses shyly, as if she was not quite certain what he would feel about them.

He took the first one from her and saw that it was Cyrilla's face painted against a blue background. Her hair was haloed by light in the manner that Frans Wyntack had made peculiarly his own.

He saw too that it was in fact an impression and not a finished portrait, and yet the huge eyes were there, with the strange, dreamy light in them, and the little straight nose.

"It is perfect!" the Marquis exclaimed. "And exactly like you!"

She gave a little laugh which he did not understand, then handed him the other canvass.

This, he saw, was a sketch of Lochner's *The Virgin of the Lilies*. The face and the expression were identical and the light came from behind as it did in the finished painting, suggesting by a few brilliant strokes a kind of celestial glory from another world which was not round the Madonna but within her.

The Marquis looked from one to the other.

"They are both excellent likenesses."

She gave another little laugh.

"The first one is not I!"

"Not you?"

"No, it is Màma. As you see, I am very like her."

"I find it difficult to believe that there are two such beautiful women in the world!" the Marquis said quietly.

"Mama was much more beautiful than I could ever be. Papa painted that when he first knew her."

"I feel you would not wish to part with it," the Marquis said reluctantly, "so if you are offering to give me anything, Miss Wyntack, I accept with the greatest pleasure this picture of you."

"I am . . . glad you like it," she said, "and I shall not feel so deeply in your debt."

With an effort the Marquis bit back the words he wanted to say, and instead remarked:

"I hardly think we can go on thanking each other over and over again, but we will talk about our gratitude tomorrow."

"There is . . . just one thing I want to . . . ask you," Cyrilla said in a low voice.

"What is that?"

"What are you going to do about the paintings? I shall be so frightened of what might happen to Papa! It would be difficult to wait until . . . tomorrow."

"I promise you, on my honour, that nothing will happen," the Marquis said. "Nothing unpleasant, at any rate. In fact, perhaps you will feel a little happier if I tell you I bought the Van Dyck at the price that was asked for it, and I shall not tell the Dealer that I have discovered it is a fake."

"Do you mean that . . . do you really mean it?" Cyrilla asked.

"I always say what I mean," the Marquis replied, "so stop worrying, and tell your maid when she returns to go out again and buy anything your father requires."

He saw the excitement on Cyrilla's face and added:

"If he is not better tomorrow, I shall suggest sending my own Physician to see him. I cannot allow you to be worried in this manner."

Again he realised that he had said more than he had intended to, and without waiting for Cyrilla's reply he opened the Studio door and started to climb somewhat carefully down the narrow stairs.

When he reached the front door the Marquis turned to take Cyrilla's hand in his.

"Let me say in all sincerity," he said quietly, "that I am very delighted to have met you, Miss Wyntack."

She curtseyed but did not look at him, and he restrained himself from kissing her hand.

Then he was outside on the pavement, and as he put his tall hat on his head, he turned back to say good-bye again before climbing into his Phaeton.

Then he saw that Cyrilla was not, as he expected, watching him go from the front door, but standing there instead was an elderly maid-servant looking at him severely and with undisguised hostility.

Chapter Three

"Miss Cyrilla!"

The voice was urgent and instantly Cyrilla was awake, raising her head from the pillow.

"What is it, Hannah?"

She knew the answer without the maid having to reply, and quickly she got out of bed, picked up her wrap which lay on a chair, slipped it on, and hurried from the room.

She had only to go next door to find Frans Wyntack's room, and as she entered it she knew without being told that he was dead.

Hannah had crossed his hands on his chest and he was lying on his back, looking, she thought, in the pale morning light like one of the warriors she had seen so often on the tombs in Churches.

In death, without the sparkle in his eyes and the smile on his lips, Frans Wyntack did in fact, with his handsome features, look almost classical, but it was different from the way Cyrilla remembered him.

Always he had been filled with gaiety and laughter, a heritage from his Austrian blood, and yet there also had been a serious side to him, which, like his painting, came from his Flemish ancestors.

She stood looking at him, thinking how handsome he was and feeling that she understood even better than she had in the past why her mother had loved him as wholeheartedly as he had loved her.

There had always been something inescapably romantic about Frans Wyntack, and something too which made him different from ordinary men because he lived in a fanciful, imaginative world all his own.

He saw everything with an artist's eye and the commonplace never seemed to encroach on him, however much Cyrilla and her mother had to face the problems of poverty and discomfort.

'He was like the Prince in a fairy-story,' Cyrilla thought now.

As if the description brought home to her forcefully that she had lost him, she went down on her knees beside the bed and tried to pray.

Inescapably it came to her mind that now Frans Wyntack and her mother would be together, and as far as they were concerned nothing else would be of any consequence.

Cyrilla was quite sure that their love was eternal and believed they would be close through all eternity. But that left her utterly alone.

She knew as she knelt there that she had been afraid of this moment ever since her mother had died, and yet she would not really have wanted to keep Frans Wyntack from the woman he loved.

Ever since he had lost her, he had seemed not to be really living but only existing; and Cyrilla, watching him, would often think that the only time he came alive was when he was painting.

She was aware that it was agony for him to sleep alone in the room he had occupied with her mother.

At night, long after she had gone to bed, she often heard him moving about the Studio and knew the reason was that he shrank from lying down alone.

'He is happy now,' she thought.

Then, because she knew how much she would miss him, the tears began to pour down her face.

*　　*　　*

The Marquis came down the stairs of his house in Berkeley Square and entered the Breakfast-Room.

The Butler and two footmen were waiting to attend to his needs. Unlike most of his contemporaries, he drank only coffee with breakfast but ate a substantial meal from the silver-crested dishes which were brought to his side for his inspection.

The hard drinking amongst the Bucks and *Beaux* of St. James's, following the example set by the Prince of Wales, had assumed such proportions that the majority of them found it impossible to rise from their beds before noon and were often not presentable until far later in the day.

But the Marquis was always rose at seven in the morning, even if he had been up late the night before, and when the streets of Mayfair were only just waking to a new day, he would be riding through them on the way to the Park to exercise one of his horses.

It was a time when he liked being alone so that he could think, and he knew he was thinking now of the same subject that had been on his mind most of the night.

When he had left Cyrilla he had driven to Carlton House, and while he was waiting for the Prince, who he was told was occupied in studying plans for alterations to his house at Brighton, he walked into the Music-Room.

It was something he had done quite often before but now his step was eager, and his eyes were more perceptive as he examined *The Virgin of the Lilies* with a new interest.

No artist, he felt, could have portrayed Cyrilla's lovely face more accurately or more delicately, and it aroused feelings in the Marquis which he had felt before and yet were now intensified to the point where they seemed completely new.

"How is it possible that anyone so perfect and so exquisite really exists?" he asked himself.

Then instantly another question presented itself.

How had he been so fortunate as to find the "Virgin of the Lilies" as unspoilt and innocent of the world as she looked in the painting?

It was then that he suddenly made the decision to keep Cyrilla to himself.

He had intended, when he left Queen Anne Terrace, to tell the Prince exactly what he had discovered, because he knew how much it would interest him.

But now he realised that if he did so, the first thing the Prince would ask was that he should meet Cyrilla.

How could he do anything else?

That, the Marquis resolved, was something he must prevent at all costs.

Never amongst the numerous women whom he had known and who had amused and entertained him had he seen one as beautiful as the Lochner Madonna, nor had he imagined that one actually existed in the flesh.

But Cyrilla was there, in that small, poverty-stricken house in Islington, and no-one was aware of it except himself.

'And that is how it must continue to be,' he decided.

He turned from the painting as the Prince entered the room behind him.

"Well, Virgo!" His Royal Highness exclaimed. "I am delighted to see you! What news have you for me?"

"Nothing very sensational, I am afraid, Sire," the Marquis replied. "I have seen Isaacs, but he is being evasive. It is not going to be easy for us to extract the information we require from him."

"That is what I was afraid you would say," the Prince said in a disappointed tone.

"To keep him quiet, Sire," the Marquis went on, "I have paid him for the Van Dyck."

"You have? That was extremely generous of you, Virgo, and of course I am very grateful."

"At the same time," the Marquis said, "I was wondering whether you would loan it to me, or the Lochner, so that I can continue my search for the truth.

I might want to show them to several people, but I think it would be a mistake for them to know that you were involved in any investigations I might make."

"Yes, yes, of course, I see your point!" the Prince agreed. "Take whichever one you wish, but do not forget that I shall want it back."

The Marquis was so pleased at the Prince's agreement that, almost without meaning to do so, he looked with delight at the Lochner painting.

"Of course," the Prince said hastily, "I would rather you took the Van Dyck, which has not yet been hung."

The Marquis was disappointed but did not show it.

"The Van Dyck it shall be, Sire," he said, "and I hope it will not be long before I can return it to you."

"When you do, of course, you will have solved the mystery about them," the Prince added.

"Of course," the Marquis agreed.

"You will dine with me?"

The Prince asked the question without much hope that the invitation would be accepted, but to his surprise the Marquis replied:

"I should be delighted to do so, Sire."

The Prince looked at him searchingly.

"You have not prevaricated. So, my instinct tells me, although I may be wrong, that last night was not a resounding success!"

The Marquis laughed.

"You are too perceptive, Sire."

The Prince linked his arm through that of his friend.

"We all have our failures," he said consolingly, "or what you call our disillusionments."

"That is true," the Marquis agreed.

He did not elaborate on the subject, for although he knew the Prince would have liked him to do so, he had made it a rule never to talk of the women on whom he bestowed his favours and he did not intend to break it now.

The Prince was right in thinking that yesterday evening had been a failure.

The Marquis had anticipated that Lady Abbott would amuse him and would prove as provocative as her gown had been at the Devonshire House party.

Unfortunately, everything that happened had a familiarity about it which made the Marquis begin to feel bored within quite a short time of arriving at Lady Abbott's mansion.

The servants had been waiting for him in the Hall, and he had known as he was escorted up the wide staircase to the first floor that he would find discreet lights, a flower-filled Boudoir, and his hostess wearing a diaphanous negligé.

"I hope you will not mind, My Lord, if we dine here tonight," she said. "I have been a little fatigued today and need to rest."

Her glance at him from her slanting eyes under her darkened eye-lashes belied the truth of her words, and it was all too obvious what she expected.

It was like the setting of a play, the Marquis thought savagely, in which he had performed the leading role a thousand times so that he was word-perfect.

Even the candlelit dinner served by silently moving servants seemed to taste the same, as did the wines, and when they were alone and there was one of those silences pregnant with meaning between them, the Marquis had an almost irresistible impulse to thank Her Ladyship for her hospitality and leave.

That he had not done so was due to the fact that he thought a scene of injured feelings, protestations, and perhaps even tears would be more than he could endure.

Instead he had played the part expected of him and gone home cursing himself for being such a fool as to have expected anything different.

"I obviously have a penchant for fakes," he told himself in the carriage driving back to Berkeley Square.

Then his thoughts were with Cyrilla again, and he knew that it was due to her and her alone that he had found the evening so banal and Lady Abbott's attractions too obvious.

He had gone to bed thinking of that small, exquisite face with its huge eyes and the expression of purity and spirituality that he had never seen before in any woman he had ever known.

He knew now that he wanted the hours to pass quickly so that he could return to Islington and see Cyrilla again, but he could hardly call on her at half-past seven in the morning, and his horse, a fine stallion which was hard to control, was waiting for him outside the front door.

He swung himself into the saddle and rode quickly towards the Park.

Having reached it, he thought the freshness of the air and even the slight mist which still hung over the Serpentine reminded him of Cyrilla.

She was as young as the morning, as fresh as the daffodils, the golden heralds of spring growing beneath the trees.

Having arrived back at Berkeley Square, the Marquis had changed his clothes and dealt with a number of letters and problems concerning his Estates presented to him by his secretary, and had at last felt free to follow his inclination to reach Islington as quickly as possible.

He drove off so intent upon his thoughts that he did not even see the raised hats of several of his male acquaintances and the wistful glances accorded him by a number of ladies.

As he passed, they were thinking that no man could look more attractive, even though, as they well knew, such attractions were dangerous to those who succumbed to them.

The Marquis reached Queen Anne Terrace in record time and, stepping down from his Phaeton, rapped sharply on the door of number 17.

There was no response for some time and he was wondering if, as had happened yesterday, Cyrilla was alone in the house while her maid had gone shopping.

Then there was the sound of a bolt being pulled back and the door opened a few inches.

It was the maid who stood there, the maid who had looked at him with disapproving eyes when he had driven away yesterday.

He recognised her as the kind of superior elderly servant who was usually to be found in far grander houses than this and in fact was the very backbone of his staff at Fane Park, where everything moved with traditional efficiency.

"Good-morning!" the Marquis said, as the maid did not speak. "I wish to see Miss Cyrilla Wyntack."

"Miss Cyrilla isn't at home!"

The words were spoken firmly, and the maid would have shut the door but the Marquis, by putting his hand on it, prevented her from doing so.

"If she is out, I will wait."

"Miss Cyrilla isn't receiving visitors," the maid said in a tone of voice which suggested that he should have understood without explanation what being "not at home" meant.

"I think she will see me," the Marquis said confidently.

"No, M'Lord!"

"I insist!"

It took a little of his strength to open the door wider, and the maid stepped back a pace with the same hostile expression he had seen before.

The Marquis waited, conscious that, as he had done before, he was using his authority without words.

As he defeated her, the maid said at length:

"If Your Lordship'll wait in the Sitting-Room, I'll tell Miss Cyrilla you're here."

The Marquis put his hat down on a chair and as the maid opened the door for him he walked into the Sitting-Room.

It seemed very small and he noticed, as he had been unable to do the day before, that the carpet was threadbare in places and the covers of the chairs had been neatly darned.

He told himself that it was not the right setting for anyone so beautiful and so perfect as Cyrilla.

'It is like seeing a perfect jewel set in pinchback instead of gold,' he thought.

He imagined the sort of background Cyrilla should have, and knew that Lochner had seen it very clearly four hundred years ago.

He heard footsteps outside the door, then she came in.

One glance at her and the Marquis knew what had happened.

He could see that she had been crying and he thought no woman could weep and look so beautiful while doing so.

Her large eyes were still misty with tears, her lips were soft, her face was very pale, and she looked, the Marquis thought, like a lily that has just been washed in the rain.

For a moment they stood looking at each other, then neither the Marquis nor Cyrilla was certain afterwards how it happened, but suddenly she was in his arms, her face hidden against his shoulder, and he could feel her whole body trembling.

"I know what has happened," the Marquis said in his deep voice.

"Papa is . . . dead! He . . . died in his . . . sleep."

The words were very low and broken, but the Marquis heard them.

"It has been a shock for you," he said gently, "but you must be brave."

"I am . . . trying to be," Cyrilla said, "but . . . every-

thing seems to have come to a . . . stop because he is
. . . no longer here."

"I think that is what we all feel when we lose
someone we love," the Marquis said.

She did not answer and he knew that she was
fighting against her tears, and his arms tightened.

"Have you arranged the Funeral?"

"N-no. Hannah said she . . . would find an Under-
taker . . . but perhaps I . . . ought to do that."

"You will do nothing of the sort," the Marquis
said. "Leave everything to me. Your father shall be
buried in the manner that you would wish. I will not
have you worrying about it and being made more
unhappy than you are already."

Cyrilla gave a little sigh and he knew it was one
of relief.

"You are . . . very kind . . . and I know it is stupid
of me . . . to feel so helpless."

The Marquis felt that she was a child whom he
must protect, and yet at the same time he was very
conscious that the soft body he held in his arms was
that of a woman.

"Come and sit down," he said. "Then I will go and
talk to your maid and tell her I will arrange everything."

"But we . . . ought not to . . . impose upon you."

She raised her head from his shoulder and looked
up at him and the Marquis thought the tears in her
eyes and on her cheeks made her even more beautiful
than she had been when she came into the room.

"You were not imposing on me," he replied, "you
are merely allowing me to do what I want to do,
which is to look after you."

For a moment she was still, then she said:

"You are . . . very kind," and moved away from
him to sit on the sofa.

With any other woman the Marquis would have
thought such an action was deliberate so that he could
sit next to her, but he knew Cyrilla's thoughts were
entirely with her dead father.

A moment later he sat beside her, but not too near, nor did he touch her.

"Is there a Church you have attended near here?" he enquired.

"Hannah and I went to Church on Sundays at St. Mary's," she replied.

"I will see the Vicar of St. Mary's and arrange that your father shall be buried in the Church-yard."

"That is what I would ... like," Cyrilla said, "but ... please ... will you ask that he should be next to ... Mama?"

"Your mother is buried there?"

"Yes."

"Then I am sure that will present no difficulties. Leave everything to me."

"How can I ... thank you? I was ... feeling so ... lost, so terribly alone ... and now ... you are here."

"Yes, I am here," the Marquis said firmly, "and so you are not lost, Cyrilla, nor are you alone. Just leave everything to me."

He saw Hannah in the kitchen before he left the house, and though he had the feeling that she was wary of him and was certainly not inclined to trust him, she was not so hostile when she learnt that he was to see to the Funeral.

At the same time, she asked:

"Why should you bother yourself, M'Lord?"

"For one reason—because as a Patron of the Arts I realise that Mr. Wyntack was an extremely accomplished artist," the Marquis answered.

"It's a pity more people didn't think so when he was alive!" Hannah remarked tartly.

"I think you will appreciate that Mr. Wyntack did not paint the sort of pictures that were likely to be popular with the type of customer that lives in this neighbourhood."

The Marquis heard her snort, but he knew she was aware that he was speaking the truth.

He put some money down on the kitchen-table.

"Buy Miss Cyrilla everything she requires."

Hannah hesitated, and, thinking she was going to refuse, he quickly said:

"I think you are both in need of nourishing food, and as I have said, I appreciated Mr. Wyntack as an artist."

Hannah knew it was an excuse so that he could help Cyrilla, but for the moment she was prepared to accept it.

"Thank you, M'Lord," she said in a not too gracious tone and dropped a curtsey.

The Marquis was smiling as he left the house to drive to the Vicarage of St. Mary's.

The Vicar was home and the Marquis told him the reason why he had called.

"I do not remember, My Lord, ever meeting Mr. Wyntack," the Cleric said, "but his daughter comes to Church with her maid every Sunday, and I buried her mother two years ago."

"May I see the grave?" the Marquis enquired.

"Of course, My Lord."

The Vicar escorted him out through a side-door into the Church-yard.

"The tombstone is a very simple one," he said. "I imagine they could not afford anything better."

The Marquis did not reply. He was reading what was inscribed:

Lorraine
Beloved of Frans Wyntack and Cyrilla
Born: 1761   Died: 1800

The tombstone was strangely worded, the Marquis thought, probably owing to the fact that Wyntack was a foreigner, but what he noticed particularly was that Cyrilla's mother had been only thirty-nine when she died.

'And she was very beautiful,' he thought, remembering the painting which Cyrilla had shown him. 'As beautiful as her daughter!'

He wished he could have seen them together.

But if Lorraine was dead Cyrilla was very much alive, and the Marquis knew that, having found her, he must never lose her again.

He made arrangements with the Vicar for the Funeral to take place within the next twenty-four hours.

He was well aware that nothing could be more upsetting than to be in a house with a corpse, and because he was prepared to pay, the Undertakers whom he saw next were ready to do anything that he asked.

The Marquis was too tactful and also too careful of Cyrilla's reputation to attend the Burial-Service.

It was unlikely that anyone would take the slightest notice of the death of an obscure and unknown artist in Islington, but one never knew.

He therefore arranged for the hearse and for a carriage for Cyrilla and Hannah, and sent a profusion of expensive flowers, but he stayed away until it was all over.

Frans Wyntack was buried with an opulence he had never known in his lifetime, and his grave was covered with wreaths which gave it a beauty he would certainly have appreciated.

As they were driving back to Queen Anne Terrace, Cyrilla said to Hannah:

"I could not . . . believe as I listened to the Service that it was . . . Papa we were burying. I felt he had . . . already left us and was . . . happy with Mama.

Hannah did not answer, but wiped a tear from the corner of her eye.

"Do you remember when Mama was alive," Cyrilla went on, "that she always seemed to know long before he opened the door that he was returning home? She would be on her feet and in the Hall, and then she would run towards him, crying:

"'Frans, oh, Frans, I have missed you! You have taken care of—yourself?'"

Cyrilla's voice broke on the words, and she went on as if she spoke to herself:

"Perhaps Mama will . . . think we did not take . . . care of him . . . properly."

"We did our best, Miss Cyrilla," Hannah said gravely.

"You were wonderful," Cyrilla said, "but he ought not to have caught the chill which made him cough all last month. We should have made certain that he put on his overcoat before he went to see the Dealers."

"He'd never listen!" Hannah said.

"Only to Mama," Cyrilla agreed.

"It's no use your reproaching yourself, Miss Cyrilla," Hannah remarked. "We did our best, and seeing how ill he was these last weeks, he'd not have wished to linger. Tossing and turning all night he was, and often talking to your mother as if he really believed she was there."

"Perhaps she . . . was," Cyrilla said beneath her breath.

Then they were home.

It was extraordinary, she thought, how the house seemed only an empty shell, and because of it she had nothing to do.

She went up to the Studio to look at Frans Wyntack's canvasses, picking up those that were nearly completed and trying to understand what he had wanted to portray with his strange splashes of light.

"The Marquis . . . understood," she told herself.

As if the thought of him conjured him up, at that moment she heard his voice in the passage, then his footsteps on the stairs.

She felt her heart leap, and when he came into the room he saw the joy in her eyes.

He seemed very big and secure, and it struck her that because he was there, the house no longer seemed empty and she was no longer lost and alone.

"Hannah tells me everything went off well," he said.

"It was a very . . . beautiful Service and the flowers were ... lovely! Thank ... you! Thank ... you!" Cyrilla replied.

"I hoped they would please you."

"They ... were for ... Papa," she said with just a note of rebuke in her voice.

"If the Church is to be believed," the Marquis replied, "there are plenty of flowers where he is at the moment, so the flowers that are given at Funerals are, I always feel, for those who are left behind."

"Whoever they were for ... it was very ... kind."

The Marquis glanced round the Studio.

"Is there anything here you want to show me?" he asked.

"You have bought one painting which Papa had nearly finished, and that was the best," Cyrilla said. "I do not think any of the others are worth even a few ... shillings."

"Suppose we are frank with each other," the Marquis said slowly, "and you start by telling me how you intend to live."

He saw by the expression on her face that this was a question she had been dreading, and that she must have asked herself what she should do almost every moment since the day her father had died.

There was silence, and as he waited for her answer the Marquis thought that the light coming through the north window made her hair, which was that strange mixture of gold and silver, appear as if it were haloed.

"You are so beautiful!" he said in a low voice. "You must realise it will not be safe for you to live alone without a man to protect you."

"I have ... Hannah."

"You cannot spend the rest of your life alone with a maid," the Marquis said, "and, sensible though she is, I cannot believe that her conversation is particularly inspiring."

His smile took the sting from his words, and almost despite herself Cyrilla smiled too.

"Hannah worries about me. She is always telling

me what I must not do, but it is difficult to ... converse with her for any length of time."

"That is what I thought," the Marquis said. "I know the Hannahs of this world well. They are very worthy but, as I have said, not particularly inspiring."

"Then where shall I find ... conversation now that ... Papa is ... dead?" Cyrilla asked.

"That is what I want to talk to you about," the Marquis replied, and as she looked at him enquiringly he said:

"I do not want to frighten you, and I know that it seems as if we have only just met each other, but that is not true. You have been in my mind and heart for a year, since I first saw you as the Madonna in *The Virgin of the Lilies*."

There was a look of astonishment in Cyrilla's eyes, then of something else which made the Marquis take a step forward and put his arms round her.

She did not resist him, and he knew that she found it as inevitable as he did that they should be close together.

Because she was different from any other woman he had known, because he felt a kind of inexplicable awe of her beauty and of the vibrations which had been aroused in him first by the painting and then by Cyrilla herself, he was very gentle.

His arms held her until, as if it were a movement of poetry or of music, he put his hand under her chin and turned her face up to his.

For a long moment he looked down at her before his lips found hers.

Everything that she did had a dream-like quality about it, and the softness of her mouth and the little tremor that he felt go through her had an unreality and yet an unmistakable magic.

To Cyrilla, the Marquis's actions were an enchantment that had carried her into a fantasy-world ever since she had first met him.

She had not known that such a man existed, and at first she had not undersrtood the strange feelings he aroused in her, and why when he was not there she still felt as if he held her close so that she could feel safe and unafraid.

Now when his lips touched hers she felt as if everything she had prayed for had come true and that in his kiss was the blessing of God and a Divine radiance that sometimes encompassed her when she was at prayer.

It was so sacred, so holy, so utterly and completely wonderful, that she could feel only as if they were enveloped by a celestial light.

The Marquis's arms tightened, but his lips were still gentle and tender and Cyrilla felt as if he drew not only her heart but her soul from her body and made it his.

'This is love,' she thought, 'love so perfect . . . so wonderful, it is what Mama . . . knew and I was . . . afraid I might never . . . find.'

But it had happened, it was here, and it was the Marquis she loved—loved so that he filled the whole world.

The Marquis raised his head.

"My darling," he exclaimed, "you belong to me! I have been searching for you all my life, and now that I have found you I can never let you go."

"I . . . love . . . you!" Cyrilla murmured.

"As I love you!" the Marquis said, and his voice was hoarse.

As he spoke, he knew the words were true; it was something he had never said before, because he had always known that if he did, it would be a lie.

But what he was feeling at this moment was love —the love he had never known.

It struck him that he, of all people, without realising it, was an idealist seeking perfection in love as he had sought it in Art and in sport and in his possessions.

And now with his incredible good luck he had found it and Cyrilla was his.

As if she understood what he was thinking, she said:

"How can we . . . feel like . . . this? I never knew . . . I . . . never dreamt when I saw you . . . outside the door, that this would . . . happen."

"And what do you think I feel?" he asked. "I used to look at your face in the painting that hangs in the Music-Room at Carlton House and think with despair that you had died centuries ago! Yet, my darling, you are real! You are here, close to me, and nothing could be more wonderful!"

Cyrilla gave a little cry.

"Suppose Papa had never . . . painted that . . . fake? Suppose you had . . . never seen . . . it? You would . . . never have come . . . looking for me."

"It was fate that we should meet," the Marquis said firmly, "and now all we have to do, my precious one, is to be grateful to the gods that have brought us together and to make sure that we are never parted."

"That . . . is what I . . . want," Cyrilla whispered.

She paused for a moment, then she said:

"Is it wrong, when Papa has only just . . . died, for me to feel . . . so marvellously . . . ecstatically . . . happy?"

"Nothing you do could be wrong," he replied, "and I am happy too in a way I never expected to be."

They sat down on a dilapidated sofa which stood against one wall of the Studio.

The Marquis put his arm round Cyrilla as he said:

"You know very little about me, darling, and I must tell you that I have a rather questionable reputation with regard to women. But that is only because I was always searching for you, only to be disillusioned over and over again."

"It does not matter," Cyrilla replied. "Mama said that when one falls in . . . love, the whole . . . world is changed . . . overnight. One is not concerned with the past, only with the future."

"Your mother was right," the Marquis said, "and therefore we will forget my past and concern ourselves only, my lovely one, with our future, when we can be together."

"Fate must have sent . . . you to me just when I . . . wanted you most," Cyrilla said. "I thought when Mama . . . died, nothing would ever be the same again and I would always be . . . miserable. But I knew I was necessary to Papa and I have to try to be happy for his sake. Yet, now . . ."

"Now?" the Marquis prompted.

"Now, when I thought I was completely . . . alone except for Hannah, and it was very frightening . . . you were . . . there! How can I ever be . . . grateful enough to God for sending . . . you to me?"

"We will be grateful together," the Marquis said with a smile. "And now, little sweetheart, let us plan the future, for I have no wish for you to stay here."

He looked at her as he said:

"I was thinking yesterday how this is not the right background for you and how much I want to give you one that is."

"Do backgrounds matter?" Cyrilla asked. "I think that wherever you were, you would be . . . yourself . . . so strong and dynamic that . . . everyone would be . . . aware of you."

"You flatter me," the Marquis replied. "My strength is as nothing compared with the beauty which makes you so outstanding. Do you realise how beautiful you are?"

"I have always . . . compared myself to . . . Mama," Cyrilla replied quite seriously, "and she was so beautiful that I am very . . . humble about . . . myself . . ."

"There is no need to be," the Marquis interrupted.

"But I want . . . you to admire . . . me," Cyrilla finished.

"This is a feeble word to describe what I feel about you," he said. "I want to give you diamonds that will frame your beauty, jewels for the rounded column of your neck, which will reflect the stars in your eyes."

"I would ... like all those ... things, but only if you want me to have them."

"I would give you the sun and the moon if it were possible," the Marquis declared. "As it is, I am a very wealthy man and you shall have everything you ever want as long as you will go on loving me."

"I shall never ... cease doing that, if we ... really belong to each ... other and you ... love me too."

"More than I can say in words," the Marquis replied.

He put his arm round her as he spoke and kissed her again, kissing her possessively and a little more passionately until, as if she was shy, she turned her face away and hid it against his shoulder.

"I will not frighten you," the Marquis said as if he admonished himself, "but, my darling, you are not only divine and ethereal but also human."

He held her close as he went on:

"I am not going to take you away from here to-night as I do not yet have a setting ready for you. By tomorrow I will find a house which you will like, with, if possible, a garden. The summer is coming and I can see you sitting amidst the flowers and under the trees. We will be alone there, and no-one will encroach on the dream-world which is ours when we are together."

"Where is this house?" Cyrilla asked. "Does it belong to you?"

"Not at the moment," the Marquis replied. "My family house in Berkeley Square, which I use when I am in London, and my ancestral house, Fane Park in Hertfordshire, are very fine. I want to show you all their treasures, especially the paintings. But in your house I shall have you entirely to myself, in a setting which is yours and yours alone, where not even my ancestors can encroach."

"It sounds ... wonderful the way you say it," Cyrilla said, "but ..."

"What is worrying you?" the Marquis asked.

"I ... I do not think I ... understand about this house."

"It will be yours," the Marquis said. "I shall give it to you and the deeds will be in your name. Whatever happens in the future, you will have somewhere to live and enough money to keep you in comfort."

He pulled her against him.

"You are mine, my little 'Virgin of the Lilies,' and I will look after you and protect you and keep you from anxiety for the rest of your life. That I swear, and, my darling, we will be happier than any two people have ever been since the beginning of time."

As he finished speaking he started to kiss her and it was impossible for her to say anything.

He kissed her until the Studio seemed to whirl round them both, and then with what was a superhuman effort he rose to his feet.

"I am going to leave you now, my precious," he said. "I want you to rest because you have been through a great deal these past few days."

Cyrilla made a little sound and he thought she was going to plead with him to stay with her, and he said quickly:

"If I do not go, nothing will be ready tomorrow. I have a great deal of planning to do, and what I intend will not be easy, but difficulties are only there for me to sweep them away."

He smiled as he added:

"I had difficulty in finding you, difficulty in getting into the house first with you and then with Hannah trying to keep me out. Now I feel I am invincible because you love me and I love you."

He pulled her to her feet, kissed her once again, then went from the Studio, and she heard her footsteps going down the stairs.

A moment later she heard the door shut behind him.

It was then that she gave a little cry which seemed to come from the very depths of her being.

Chapter Four

Cyrilla stood staring at the door as if she thought the Marquis would come back or she must run after him.

Then with a murmur that was somehow infinitely pathetic she put her hands over her face.

She was crying helplessly when Hannah came into the Studio.

"I was just wondering..." she was saying; then as she looked at Cyrilla, she moved forward and said:

"What's the matter? What has upset you?"

"Oh, Hannah! Hannah! How was... I did not ... know!"

As if she must have something or someone to protect her, Cyrilla turned to the maid and put her face against her breast.

She was crying despairingly by this time and Hannah asked again:

"What's the matter? What has upset you? You were so brave at the Funeral."

"It... is not... Papa."

"Then what's His Lordship done?"

There was a sharpness in Hannah's voice now, and as she held Cyrilla in her arms, as she had done since she was a baby, there was a fiercely protective look in her eyes.

At the same time there was the anger and suspi-

71

cion which the Marquis had seen when he first saw her
outside the door before he drove away.

"What has His Lordship said to you? Tell me!"
Hannah insisted.

"I thought he . . . loved . . . me."

"He appeared to do so!"

"I . . . believed in him . . . I believed that he loved
me . . . as I loved him."

Cyrilla's voice was almost incoherent, but Hannah
was only too well aware of what she was saying, and
before she could reply Cyrilla went on:

"How could I . . . suffer as Mama . . . suffered?
How could I . . . live like . . . that all over again? I
could not . . . bear it, Hannah . . . not even . . . with him
. . . and I love . . . him . . . love him with . . . all my
heart!"

"That's not love, Miss Cyrilla, as you well know,
not from a gentleman who has only seen you three or
four times at the most. Now stop crying and listen to
me."

Hannah spoke not as a maid would speak but as a
Nanny, and it was as her Nurse that Cyrilla made an
effort to obey her.

Hannah moved her back a step or two and sat
her down in an arm-chair; then, standing beside her,
with her arms crossed, she said:

"I told you when your mother died that you
should go where you belong, but you wouldn't listen
to me."

"How . . . could I? You know what a . . . state Papa
was . . . in. I had to . . . stay with him. I *had* to! It was
. . . what Mama would have . . . wanted."

"Well, he's now no longer here," Hannah said,
"and I'll listen to no more excuses. I wanted to say
this to you as soon as the Funeral was over, but His
Lordship was here before I had a chance."

The mere mention of the Marquis made Cyrilla's
tears flow afresh, and she said in an almost inaudible
voice:

"I . . . love him, Hannah . . . but I . . . cannot do . . . what he . . . asks."

"I should think not indeed!" Hannah agreed indignantly. "He deceived me as he deceived you with his kindness over the Master's Funeral, his flowers, and his money."

Cyrilla raised her head.

"Hannah! You have . . . not taken . . . money from . . . him?"

"Only a few pounds, Miss Cyrilla, to buy food, and that's something that can easily be paid back once you do what's right and proper."

"Is it . . . right and . . . proper?" Cyrilla asked. "Supposing . . . supposing . . ."

"There's no supposing about it!" Hannah said sharply. "I'm taking you to Holm House immediately, so stop crying. Put on your cape."

"Im-immediately?" Cyrilla stammered.

"What's the point of waiting?" Hannah asked. "In fact, this is what I intended to do as soon as you had recovered."

Cyrilla gave a deep sigh.

"I do not know . . . what to say . . . Hannah, and I do not . . . know what . . . to do."

"Well, I do!" Hannah said. "And that's why, Miss Cyrilla, we'll have no more arguments. I must do what's right, and if you'll not come with me, I'll have to go alone."

Cyrilla looked at her with a startled expression.

"Do not . . . leave me . . . alone . . . I cannot stay . . . here, in case . . ."

They both knew she was afraid that the Marquis might return, and if he did, Cyrilla thought, she would be unable to refuse anything he asked of her.

As if she understood what Cyrilla was feeling, Hannah put out her hand and drew her to her feet.

"Come along," she said, "there's no time to be lost."

"How . . . are you . . . sure?" Cyrilla tried to say,

but Hannah had already left the Studio and was walking down the narrow passage to her bedroom.

She came back a moment later with Cyrilla's warm cloak and put it over her shoulders.

"Perhaps I . . . should wear a . . . bonnet," Cyrilla suggested in a far-away voice.

"There's no need," Hannah replied. "You come just as you are. It's getting chilly now that the sun is going down."

She fastened the cape under Cyrilla's chin and started to walk down the stairs.

"Our clothes . . . should we not . . . take them?" Cyrilla asked.

"We've plenty of time to fetch them if they are needed," Hannah answered.

She walked to the kitchen and took down her bonnet and shawl from a hook on the back of the door and put them on.

She went back to where Cyrilla was waiting at the bottom of the stairs and, passing her, opened the front door.

"Wait!" Cyrilla cried. "I want . . . time to . . . think! We must not do . . . anything we shall . . . regret."

"The only thing we shall regret is if we stay here," Hannah replied. "As I've said before, Miss Cyrilla, you are going to where you ought to be, and no amount of talk can make that anything but right and what you should do."

As she spoke, she stepped onto the pavement and waited for Cyrilla.

Slowly, clutching her handkerchief wet with tears, Cyrilla followed, and, having pulled the door shut behind her, Hannah turned the key in the lock and put it in the pocket in the seam of her gown.

Standing on the edge of the pavement, she watched the traffic passing by.

It was not long before a hackney-carriage appeared; the elderly coachman, driving a tired horse in an indifferent fashion, was not making much effort to look out for a passenger.

Hannah waved at him and it took a few seconds before she could attract his attention. Then he drew his horse to a standstill.

"Come along, Miss Cyrilla," Hannah said sharply.

Cyrilla, deep in her thoughts, was barely aware of what was happening.

Hannah helped her into the carriage but before she followed her she said to the coachman:

"Holm House in Park Lane."

For a moment the coachman seemed surprised, as if he had not expected such an important address. Then he raised his hand to the brim of his hat and said:

"Very good, Ma'am."

Hannah sat beside Cyrilla and they drove for a while in silence. Then she said quietly:

"You've got to make yourself pleasant, and remember, we've nowhere else to go."

Cyrilla did not answer.

She was thinking that there was a house waiting for her, had she accepted it—a house with a garden where she could sit amongst the flowers and trees and where she could be alone with the Marquis.

She shut her eyes and felt again his lips on hers when he had carried her up into the sky, and she thought that no-one could know such wonder and ecstasy and yet be alive.

His kisses had been everything she had imagined a kiss should be, and so much more, just as his love had been so perfect that it personified all her dreams and everything she had ever imagined love was.

And yet when she had understood what he was offering her, she had known it was not a love that she wanted, not a love that she could even contemplate, but something from which she shrank in horror.

She must have made a little murmur of pain, for Hannah said solicitously:

"It's hard, Miss Cyrilla. I know that. Don't think I've not suffered all the years I was with your mother, seeing her grow weaker and more wan every day from lack of food, and knowing she had thrown away everything that made life comfortable and decent."

"She ... never regretted ... it," Cyrilla murmured.

"That's as may be!" Hannah retorted. "And I'm not saying she did regret anything for herself, but she regretted for you. Many a time she said to me: 'This life is not right for Cyrilla, Hannah.'"

"I was very happy with Mama ... and ... Papa," Cyrilla said almost defiantly, as if she could not bear Hannah to disparage in any way her mother's behaviour.

"Your mother was well aware, as I was, that you should have had children to play with, parties to go to, and ponies to ride," Hannah said.

"None of ... those things were ... important, because I was with ... Mama."

Hannah opened her lips to speak, then closed them again, and Cyrilla knew that she forced herself not to say that her mother was at times barely aware of her existence.

From the very first she had known that Frans Wyntack was her mother's whole world. He was all she had ever wanted, and everything and everybody else, even her daughter, was of little consequence.

Cyrilla had not been jealous. She had only felt left out, and it was then that she would slip away from the Sitting-Room to sit in the kitchen with Hannah, talking to her, watching her cook, and aware that here at least she mattered.

She knew, if she was honest, that without Hannah her life would have been a very dreary one.

It was Hannah who took her for walks, gave her good books to read; and, when they had a little money, took her to Concerts and, on one unforgettable occasion, to the Theatre to see one of William Shakespeare's plays.

It was Hannah who—again, when they could afford it—insisted that Cyrilla had teachers to instruct her in English and French, and any other subjects which were beyond her ability to teach.

The lessons were intermittent, but at the same time, because Cyrilla was so attentive, so keen to learn, many of the teachers would come even when they were not paid.

It was entirely due to Hannah that Cyrilla's education had not been as neglected as it might have been.

Now, apprehensively, Cyrilla thought of her ignorance of any type of life except the one which she had known within the confines of the small house in Islington.

There had always been Mama to talk to when Frans Wyntack was too busy painting to want them in the Studio or had gone out to try to sell his paintings.

Mama was so knowledgeable that Cyrilla had often thought she could teach her more in an hour than a dozen teachers could do in a month.

Mama could speak French perfectly, also Italian. Mama could play the piano and sing extracts from the Operas.

Mama had read books on almost every subject and she could explain about paintings and Art even better than Frans Wyntack could.

Yet Cyrilla was aware that there were great gaps in her education, and for the first time since she had fallen in love with him, she thought that perhaps the Marquis might, in time, find her a bore.

What did she know of his life? And although he had said: "We will make sure we are never parted," how could she believe him?

'Hannah is right,' she thought despairingly.

Yet she felt the tears come into her eyes and it was impossible to force them away, impossible to speak.

They drove on in silence until the mean streets gave way to wider and more fashionable ones. They reached Mayfair and turned down Park Lane.

It was then that Cyrilla said:

"I am sure we are making a ... mistake, Hannah. Let us go ... back. If the Marquis calls, we will not

... let him in. You and I will manage on our own."

"And do you think you could keep His Lordship out?" Hannah asked.

The words were like a splash of cold water against her face, Cyrilla thought, and she knew it would be impossible for either of them to keep the Marquis out of the house and out of her life.

Despairingly she thought that perhaps she was being foolish in fighting against the man she loved and giving up the heavenly joy she found in his arms.

Yet even as she thought of him she saw her mother, thin and emaciated, her eyes dull except when Frans Wyntack was there, and she knew she could not contemplate allowing that to happen to herself.

Besides, if she ever fell into the condition that her mother had, it was unlikely that the Marquis would stay with her.

"We're here!"

Hannah's voice broke in on her thoughts and Cyrilla clenched her hands together with an effort at self-control.

"Leave everything to me," Hannah said briskly, "and just remember that there's no alternative. This is what you have to do and what your mother would want, if you could ask her."

The coachman, who was obviously impressed by the fine house to which he had brought his passengers, stepped down and opened the door for them.

Cyrilla, however, gave it only a perfunctory glance before she followed Hannah, who, having paid the cabman, had walked up the steps to the front door.

Before she could raise her hand to the knocker the door was opened by a footman wearing a powdered wig and a livery of dark blue and yellow with crested silver buttons.

"Is His Grace at home?" Hannah enquired.

"Have you an appointment, Ma'am?"

"We wish to see His Grace," Hannah said firmly.

"His Grace's seeing no-one he's not expecting," the footman announced.

Special Membership

HEALTH AND HAPPINESS CLUB

$8.50 VALUE

As a new member, we will rush you your SPECIAL FREE BONUS of Barbara Cartland's "Look Lovely" Moisturizer.

Dear Barbara,

Kindly enroll me as a New Member in your Health And Happiness Club. I enclose my one-year membership fee of only $5.00 payable to Health And Happiness Club Inc., Two Penn Plaza, New York, N.Y. 10001.

Please rush your first newsletter and my special free bonus. My membership fee is enclosed by:

Money Order ☐   Check ☐

or charge to my

Master Charge ☐   Visa ☐

Card No. _____ Exp. Date _____

Signature _____

Name _____

Address _____ Apt. No. _____

City _____

State _____ Zip _____

"Is Mr. Burton here?" Hannah enquired.

The footman looked surprised at the question and glanced over her shoulder.

As he did so, Hannah stepped into the Hall.

"Fetch Mr. Burton, if you please."

The footman, who was young and somewhat inexperienced, stood, indecisive, as Cyrilla slowly entered the Hall behind Hannah.

It was large and rather dark in the evening light which came through two stained-glass windows, and Cyrilla felt herself shiver and knew she was nervous.

Then at the far end of the Hall, from under the stairs, an elderly Butler, white-haired and somewhat pontifical in appearance, came walking towards them.

He was about to ask what was happening, then looked at Hannah with an incredulous expression on his face.

"Good-evening, Mr. Burton," Hannah said.

"Miss Hannah! I wasn't expecting to see you!" the Butler exclaimed.

"His Grace is here, I understand?"

Hannah did not wait for a reply. She merely turned to Cyrilla and started to undo her cloak at the neck.

"It's warm in here, you won't need this," she said.

Cyrilla felt as if she were only a baby in the maid's hands and made no protests as the cloak was taken from her and given to the footman, who, having closed the front door, was standing there listening.

There was no doubt that Cyrilla's appearance surprised the Butler.

He stared at her for a long moment without speaking. Then he said to Hannah in a voice that was barely above a whisper:

"You've brought her back to His Grace?"

Hannah nodded.

The eyes of the two servants met and it seemed as if a message of understanding passed between them without there being any necessity for words.

The Butler turned and started to walk across the

Hall, and Cyrilla would not have followed him had not Hannah put out her arm and moved her forward.

Automatically she walked behind the elderly man until he opened a door and said, raising his voice a trifle:

"A lady to see Your Grace!"

As if it was something she remembered doing in the past, Cyrilla walked past him. Then as she heard the door close behind her she knew that she was alone and Hannah had not accompanied her.

At the far end of a somewhat sombre room lined with books sat a man in a wing-backed arm-chair in front of a fire.

For a moment he did not move, then he turned his head and Cyrilla saw him suddenly become rigid as if transfixed.

"Lorraine!"

Cyrilla could barely heard the word, yet she understood.

She walked forward, feeling that her heart was beating tumultuously, her lips were dry, and her hands were trembling.

She drew near him and the man in the chair watched her as if he was unable to take his eyes from her. Then he said in a harsh voice:

"You must be Cyrilla!"

"Yes ... Papa."

"I thought you were your mother."

"Mama is ... dead."

"Dead?"

The words were little more than a gasp and she knew it had been a shock to him.

"When did she die?"

"Two years ago."

"Why?"

"She grew ... weaker and ... weaker through ... lack of food."

If she had meant to startle the man in the chair she had certainly succeeded.

"What are you saying to me?"

"We did not ... have enough ... money to eat ... properly."

There was an expression in the Duke's eyes that she thought was one of pain, and after a moment he said:

"Is that why you have come home now?"

"Yes ... Papa."

"Why did you not come after your mother died?"

"If I had ... Frans Wyntack would have ... killed himself, and I think she would have ... wanted me to look ... after him." ·

"What has happened to him now?"

"He died ... yesterday ... so Hannah brought ... me to you."

"Hannah is still with you?"

"Yes ... Papa. She is ... outside in the ... Hall."

"And you really think I would take you back, seeing the life you have been leading with your mother and—that man?"

The Duke's voice was suddenly harsh. It sounded to Cyrilla like the crack of a whip, and it broke her self-control.

She gave a muttered cry and rushed forward to throw herself on her knees in front of him.

"Let me come to you, Papa. Please ... let me stay with you," she begged, her words tumbling over one another. "I have ... no money and nowhere else to ... go ... unless I do what I know is wrong ... and that I cannot ... contemplate, even though I ... I love him. ..."

Because the words brought back to her mind the agony of losing the Marquis, she burst into tears.

Now she bent her head and laid it against the Duke's knee and cried despairingly as a child would do who has lost security and everything that means love and comfort in its life.

Then she felt the Duke's hand on her head, stroking her hair, and it was strangely comforting.

"Who is this man?"

She heard his voice as if it came from a long distance, and as she groped for the handkerchief which she had put in her sash when they entered the house, the Duke took a fine linen one from his pocket and put it into her hands.

It was soft and smelt of lavender and Cyrilla pressed it against her eyes, trying to stop her tears.

"Suppose you tell me what has upset you," the Duke suggested in a very different tone of voice from the one he had used before.

"I ... believed when he said he ... loved me that he ... meant it," Cyrilla began.

There was a note of self-disparagement in her voice which the Duke did not miss.

"You are saying," he went on in the same quiet tone, "that this man did not offer you marriage?"

"No ..."

"That is not surprising, considering—"

The Duke checked himself from saying more, but Cyrilla knew only too well what he had been about to say.

"He ... did not ... know about Mama," she said hastily. "Nobody knew ... and there were few people to know ... as we had no ... friends."

"That was your mother's choice," the Duke said, and now his voice was harsh again, "but we are talking about you. Who is this man? And if you had no friends, how did you meet him?"

"He came to the ... house about a ... painting."

"And his name?"

"He is the Marquis of ... F-Fane."

She felt the Duke stiffen and after a moment he said:

"Fane? Fane! What has Fane to do with you? That rake—that ravisher of women! He is not the sort of man I would allow my daughter to associate with."

"I ... I love him ... Papa ... I cannot help it ... it is just ... something that ... happened."

"It is something that should not have happened!" the Duke said. "In no circumstances—and make no mistake about it, Cyrilla—will I allow him to set foot in any house that belongs to me!"

There was silence for a moment, then Cyrilla asked:

"Does that mean ... Papa ... that I may ... stay here?"

The Duke did not reply and she added pathetically:

"It is ... the only way I can ... avoid seeing him ... please ... Papa ... let me ... stay?"

"If you stay here," the Duke said after a moment, "it will not be because you are hiding from the Marquis of Fane, but because you are my daughter. I have often thought, Cyrilla, that I was wrong in allowing your mother to take you with her."

"She left Edmund with you. How ... how is he?"

"He is in Europe at the moment, doing the 'Grand Tour,'" the Duke replied, "but all these years I have missed my daughter."

"Oh ... Papa ... is that ... true?"

"It is true."

Cyrilla looked up at the Duke and thought there was an expression in his eyes that was one of inexpressible pain.

After a moment she said in a whisper:

"You have ... mised Mama ... too."

The Duke stirred a little uncomfortably in his chair.

"Your mother left me, and I will not talk about it."

"I understand, Papa, but although she was happy ... very happy with ... Frans Wyntack, I think she missed ... you and Edmund more than she would ever ... admit."

"I do not want to hear any more," the Duke said harshly. "I want you to tell me about yourself."

Cyrilla gave him a little smile, and as there were still tears on her cheeks it was like the sunshine after rain.

"There is really ... nothing to ... tell," she said.

"We lived in a very small house in Islington which Hannah always disliked, and it was fun until Mama became . . . ill. After that . . . everything was really very . . . very miserable."

The Duke looked at her for a moment, then rose to his feet to stand in front of the fire while Cyrilla sat back on her heels, looking up at him.

"Damn the man!" he ejaculated. "He ruined my life and he has ruined yours!"

"Not . . . really, Papa," Cyrilla said.

At the same time, she could understand what her father was feeling.

When her mother died she had said to Hannah as she wept:

"This is how Papa must have . . . felt when Mama ran away from him. He must have been desperately . . . unhappy, knowing that she could . . . never come back."

She thought now the Duke looked very much older than she remembered him.

It was, of course, eight years since she had last seen him. Even so, his hair was now dead-white and the lines on his face were deeply etched.

He must be sixty, Cyrilla thought, but he looked older and she knew perceptively that the last vestige of his youth must have ebbed away when her mother left him for Frans Wyntack.

Because she could understand how much he had suffered and because she wanted to comfort him, she said:

"If . . . I may stay with you . . . Papa . . . perhaps we can be happy . . . together. I have missed you . . . as you have missed me."

The Duke smiled and it broke the severity of his expression.

"It will make me happy to have you with me, Cyrilla," he said. "You may, however, find me difficult to live with, for I have grown set in my ways and I find it hard to make changes."

"I will try not to ask for . . . any," Cyrilla promised, "and now I know Hannah was right and I . . . belong with . . . you."

"I am glad you think that," the Duke said. "You have grown very lovely in these last years. In fact, you look exactly like your—"

He broke off as if he could not bear to say any more, and Cyrilla rose to her feet to stand beside him.

"It is difficult . . . not to talk of . . . Mama," she said, "and ever since I have seen you I have had a feeling . . . a very strong feeling . . . that she would want us to be . . . together . . . just as Hannah was sure . . . that that was what she . . . would want."

"I had better see Hannah," the Duke said. "It appears to me she is the only person who has shown any sense in this whole regrettable affair."

Cyrilla gave a little smile.

"Hannah is always sensible, and when I am with her I feel I have never grown up. She is still thinking I am in the Nursery and should be quietly playing with my toys."

A faint smile twisted the Duke's lips.

Hannah had been maid to his wife when he had married her, and the only thing that had prevented him from worrying over the well-being of his daughter all these years was the knowledge that Hannah was there to look after her as she had always looked after his wife.

The Duke was not a violent man, and all his life he had been self-controlled and had found it difficult to express his inner feelings.

Yet, when his wife had run away with an obscure and unknown artist, he had hated the man with a violence that was almost murderous.

Most other men would have challenged Frans Wyntack to a duel, and, having either killed him or brought him near death, would then have forced his wife to return to him.

But the Duke was acutely conscious of his position and the scandal that such action would evoke.

He was thinking not only of himself but of his

son when he decided that the best thing he could do was to ignore what had happened and not even admit that his wife had left him for another man.

For a long time he answered all enquiries about the Duchess by saying that she was staying abroad with friends.

When the war with France made this impossible, he said instead that she was in Ireland because she enjoyed the hunting there.

Because the Duke was a very unapproachable person, no-one was prepared to challenge such a statement, but at the same time there was, amongst his relatives and friends, a great deal of speculation as to what had happened.

No-one knew the truth, although there were a great number of people who said that because the Duchess was so many years younger than her husband, it would not be surprising if she had lost her heart to a younger man.

But he fact remained that no-one knew the truth, and gradually, because there were other, more interesting things to talk about, people stopped speculating about the disappearance of the Duchess and her daughter.

When the older ladies of the Holmbury family were brave enough to ask the Duke point-blank how long the Duchess intended to stay away and shirk her responsibilities, they received no answer.

Instead they felt only that they had antagonised their formidable relative, which was something that must not happen again.

The Duke put out his hand towards the bell-pull.

"I will see Hannah now," he said. "And I imagine the first thing you will need is some new clothes."

"That is true, Papa," Cyrilla agreed, "but please do not let me be . . . seen anywhere in . . . London."

"If you are afraid of meeting the Marquis of Fane," the Duke replied, "I can put your mind at rest by telling you that the circles in which I move would not accept such a scallywag, even though his horses do win the best races!"

There was still a look of anxiety on Cyrilla's face, and he went on after a moment:

"To set your mind at rest, Cyrilla, we will return to the country. My attendance at Court is not really required and there are always plenty of other people to take my place."

"I would not ... want to upset your ... plans, Papa."

"It will certainly not upset me," he said. "I dislike London as I always have. As soon as you are dressed as befits your position as my daughter, we will go to the Castle. I think you will find it very much as you remember it."

"I hope so! I hope it has not changed!" Cyrilla cried. "I cannot tell you how often I have dreamt of riding on my pony in the Park, climbing up to tower to look at the view from the battlements, and feeding the goldfish in the herb-garden."

The Duke smiled and put his arm round her shoulder.

"They are all just the same," he said, "and we will look at them together."

"I will like that, Papa."

The door opened and Burton stood there.

There was a smile in his old eyes when he saw father and daughter standing together.

"Bring Hannah in to me, Burton," the Duke said.

"I'll do that, Your Grace, and may I say it's a real pleasure to have Lady Cyrilla back with us."

The Duke did not reply, and Cyrilla made a little sound that was not unlike a sob.

"I had ... forgotten I was 'Lady' Cyrilla! Oh ... Papa ..."

She stopped herself from saying any more, because impulsively, almost forgetting to whom she was speaking, she had been about to say that she wondered whether the Marquis would have offered her marriage if he had known who she really was.

She thought it was the sort of question which she ought not to ask herself, and yet it persisted all the time that the Duke was talking to Hannah.

She was taken upstairs to one of the best bedrooms while a footman was sent post-haste to Bond Street to instruct the best dressmakers, from whom her mother had bought her gowns in the past, to call first thing in the morning.

Cyrilla looked round the bedroom and thought she had forgotten how comfortable and attractive a room could be in one of her father's houses.

She had very seldom come to London as a child and so she recalled very little about Holm House, but she had felt it was unlikely that she would be disappointed when she saw it.

Hannah and the Housekeeper, rustling in black silk, were fussing over the things she required.

"There's no need to fetch anything tonight from where you've been living, Miss Hannah," the Housekeeper was saying. "I can find Her Ladyship a nightgown, and tomorrow it'll be easy to purchase everything she requires."

"I'm sure that will be a pleasure, Mrs. Kingdom," Hannah said.

When the Housekeeper left the room, Cyrilla said:

"When you go back to the house, Hannah, I will make a list of what I want you to bring me."

"There's nothing there you'll want in the future, M'Lady," Hannah said determinedly.

"There must be some things," Cyrilla replied. "Perhaps a painting . . ."

"Forget those paintings!" Hannah snapped. "They've brought nothing but trouble and misery. If I had my way, I'd make a bonfire of the lot!"

"Hannah!" Cyrilla exclaimed. "I had no idea you felt like that!"

"What was the point of saying so when we had enough to worry about as it was?" Hannah retorted. "But it was pictures that brought that man into your mother's life, pictures which would not sell and which brought us near to starvation, pictures that made His Lordship come a-knocking at the door!"

"And a picture of me," Cyrilla said in a very small voice. "I did not tell you, Hannah, but Frans Wyntack painted me in two ... fakes which the Dealer took to the Prince of Wales. Of course, it was obvious he would think it strange that two artists one hundred fifty years apart should have painted the same model."

"That's just the kind of stupid thing that would happen!" Hannah snapped. "Well, it's all over now, and you've just got to forget all about it. Those years have been a penance for me, I can tell you, thinking of everything that your mother was missing, and you."

"You were very kind to us both," Cyrilla said softly, "and now that I know how terribly you hated it, I am sorry, Hannah. And I am glad for your sake that it is over."

"Yes, it's over, M'Lady!" Hannah said firmly. "There will be no going back, no regrets, and no hankering after His Lordship. You know as well as I do that His Grace wouldn't stand for that."

"Papa said some very ... unkind things about ... him," Cyrilla said, almost as if she spoke to herself.

"And with good reason," Hannah said.

"You did not tell me you disapproved of him when he came to the house," Cyrilla said.

"I thought he meant to help us," Hannah replied. "All I can tell you, M'Lady, is that you've had a lucky escape, a very lucky escape!"

As Hannah busied herself arranging a bath for Cyrilla and having the gown in which she had arrived pressed because she had nothing else to put on for dinner, Cyrilla stood at the window looking out over the grey roofs.

Twilight was falling and the sky was grey too, and she suddenly felt an intense longing to hear the Marquis's voice talking to her in the garden where they would sit together and in the little house where they would be alone.

Then she told herself that, as Hannah had said, she had to put all that behind her.

She loved him, but what he had asked of her was impossible, and she knew only too well that it was a life in which she would be ostracised by Society, a life in which everything was sacrificed for the love of a man.

Looking back, she could remember how it had been when her mother first ran away, how she had been afraid to leave the house just in case she should meet someone she knew and be recognised.

"No-one in this place will be expecting to see the Duchess of Holmbury," Frans Wyntack had said.

"One can never be too sure."

"I am sure! And what do you think I feel, my darling, when I know I have made you ashamed of your very existence?"

"I would never be ashamed of you," the Duchess had replied. "It is just that I am afraid that if he knew where we were, my husband would take his revenge on you."

"That was the risk I took when I asked you if our love meant more than rank and wealth and all the other things he could give you."

"Yes, but suppose he wounded you or even killed you? Then my life would be over too."

She had not realised that Cyrilla was listening and watching as Frans Wyntack put his arms round her mother and drew her close against him.

Then as he began to kiss her passionately she had slipped away, hurrying downstairs to the kitchen where Hannah would talk, in her sane, sensible voice, of ordinary things.

Always they had to be surreptitious and careful, and when her mother took her to Church she wore a thick veil over her face.

"People will think it strange that you hide your face in such a way, Mama," Cyrilla had said.

"Perhaps they will think I am so ugly that I am afraid for anyone to look at me," her mother had said with a smile, "or that I have bad skin."

"But you are beautiful, Mama, and it gives people pleasure to look at anything lovely."

Her mother had not answered, and Cyrilla had been well aware that people looked at them curiously when they sat in the small, obscure pew in the back of the Church and slipped out the moment the Service was over.

It was Hannah who went shopping with Cyrilla.

"Where shall we deliver the goods, Ma'am?" the shop-keepers would ask.

"I'll take them with me," Hannah would reply firmly.

Cyrilla knew that they thought it was strange and that their estimation went down because they did not require the ordinary service that everyone expected.

There was not one but a thousand little pin-pricks to make her acutely conscious that they were outcasts.

If people came to the door asking for money for charity, or even on one or two occasions calling because they were new to the neighbourhood, her mother would rush upstairs and hide in her bedroom and Hannah would say firmly that neither Mr. nor Mrs. Wyntack was at home.

Occasionally, after they had been living in the house for a year or so, Frans Wyntack would bring home some fellow-artists.

It was then, as Cyrilla grew older, that she sensed something which shocked and humiliated her. These men, because they either knew or suspected that Frans Wyntack was not married, spoke to her mother with a familiarity which her father would not have tolerated for one second.

They were not rude, for they would certainly never have been that to anyone so beautiful; it was just something in the way they spoke and the tone of their voices, and most of all in the look in their eyes, which Cyrilla detested.

It was a lack of courtesy and certainly of the awe with which her mother was approached when she lived in the Castle as the Duchess of Holmbury.

People's attitude to a Duchess was very different from what it was to a woman who was living in an artist's house and had a daughter who was not his.

"Never, never, never," Cyrilla had said to herself over and over again, when one of these little incidents had hurt her, "will I put myself in the same position. One day I will be married, and I will be respectable."

She did not add that she never would run away, but she thought it, and although she could understand that the love her mother felt for Frans Wyntack was for her overwhelming and compelling and in a way irresistible, to Cyrilla it was an emotion which she would never feel but which if she did she would suppress and behave conventionally.

Sometimes she missed her brother in a manner that made her long to suggest that she go home and see him.

"Edmund will be seventeen today," her mother had said when Cyrilla was fifteen. "I would like to see him and wish him Many Happy Returns of the Day!"

"I expect that is what he is longing for you to do, Mama," Cyrilla replied.

There was a far-away look in her mother's eyes, which Cyrilla knew meant she was thinking of her son, whom Cyrilla had often thought her mother loved more than she loved her.

Because she wanted more than she dared express to be with Edmund on his birthday, she had left her mother's bedroom and gone downstairs to Hannah.

"What do you think Edmund is doing today, Hannah?" she had asked.

"Counting his presents, I shouldn't wonder," Hannah retorted. "And that's more than you were able to do on your birthday."

"Mama says she will give me something very nice as soon as we have some money."

"And when will that be, I'd like to know?" Hannah questioned, rolling out some pastry in an aggressive manner which told Cyrilla that she was annoyed.

"I expect Edmund will have a new horse for his birthday," Cyrilla went on, following her thoughts. "He always wanted horses more than anything else. I used to love riding with him when he would take me. I wish I could ride with him today!"

"If wishes were horses, beggars would ride!" Hannah said. "And that's what we are—beggars! It's something I never expected in all my born days!"

It was not much consolation talking to Hannah after all, and Cyrilla had gone into the Sitting-Room to think about Edmund and imagine him galloping over the Park on a new horse.

His fair hair would be blowing in the wind because as usual he would forget to wear a hat, and he would be teasing her because she could not keep up with him on her pony, which had always been smaller than his.

'What fun it used to be!' she thought with a little sob.

Then she had been ashamed of herself because, as she told herself every day and every night, she was so lucky to have Mama all to herself while Edmund had been left with Papa.

She was well aware that she was fortunate, for Frans Wyntack had always been very kind to her, and she had called him "Papa" because it had pleased her mother.

"He *is* your father now, darling," her mother had said. "It makes him happy to think you are his little daughter when he is unable to have one of his own."

"Why is he not able to have one, Mama?" Cyrilla had asked.

It was several years later that she realised that because her mother and Frans Wyntack were not married they would not think of bringing children into the world when they could not give them a name.

This was another reason which made Cyrilla know that never in any circumstances would she put herself in the same position as her mother had.

'I would like lots of sons like Edmund,' she thought when she was alone in her little room at night, 'and it would be nice for me if I had sisters I could play with.'

But she knew, because she was hypersensitive, that those who came to the house were very careful not to talk to her about her real father.

In some way they knew that she was not really Frans Wyntack's child, and it gradually became clear that they thought that her father, whoever he might have been, did not acknowledge her.

Therefore, as she had been born out of wedlock, they considered it best not to speak of him, but to refer to Frans Wyntack as her father.

In a way, it was the final humiliation of her position and her mother's.

"How could they think such things of Mama?" she had asked herself.

Then, because Hannah had taught her a little of her own common sense, she knew it would have been strange if they had thought or done anything else.

"I hate it! I hate this life!" she would say sometimes in the secrecy of her bedroom.

And yet it was the very same life which the Marquis had asked her to share with him.

"We will be together, my darling," he had said, and it was something she had heard Frans Wyntack say often enough.

"What does anything matter, as long as we are *together*? Why should we worry about tomorrow when we are *together* today? We must forget the past. All that matters is that we are *together*, you and I."

She could hear him saying such words over and over again in his attractive voice, which still had a foreign accent, and always her mother responded, always her eyes lit up, because she loved him.

It was then that Cyrilla had known that "being *together*" would not be enough for her. She wanted everything else as well—security, propriety, respectability, and marriage!

Chapter Five

The Marquis drove towards Islington with a smile on his lips.

He had the same triumphant feeling as when he had won a race or beaten his opponent at boxing.

He had in fact achieved what his secretary had told him was impossible, and he was quite justifiably pleased with himself.

When yesterday afternoon he had gone back to Fane House to send for Mr. Ashworth, his secretary, whose duties were similar to those of a Royal Comptroller, he had felt that planning a home for Cyrilla was the most exciting thing he had ever done in his whole life.

It would be impossible, he realised, to provide her immediately with everything he wanted for her.

But already as he drove away from Islington he had been thinking of the paintings with which he would embellish her house, the carpets which would cover the floors, and the furniture which would give her the type of background that was worthy of her beauty.

He had already decided that she should be surrounded by paintings that would make her loveliness even more pronounced than Lochner had managed to do, and he decided that a Boucher and a Botticelli which hung at Fane Park should be moved to her house when he found it for her.

When he said to his secretary:

"I want you to buy, today, a house near here which is architecturally outstanding and also has a garden," Mr. Ashworth had stared at him in astonishment.

"Today, My Lord?"

"Today!" the Marquis said firmly.

"But it is not possible."

"Nothing is impossible!" the Marquis replied. "Not where I am concerned."

He smiled as he spoke, and Mr. Ashworth thought that something had obviously pleased his Master, for he had never seen him look so happy or indeed so sure of himself.

He wondered what could have happened.

There had been no race-meeting in which the Marquis's horses would have come in first as usual, and that was the only sporting-event in which he was actively engaged.

And yet he undoubtedly had the appearance of a winner.

Mr. Ashworth was, however, far too tactful to make personal remarks. Instead he said:

"I will do my best, My Lord, to find the house you require, but I cannot be over-optimistic, for the Season has just started and houses that were unoccupied have now been let for at least the next two months."

"Look, Ashworth! Look!" the Marquis ordered.

"I have two letters here for you to sign, My Lord," Mr. Ashworth said, as if he was relieved to change the subject, "and also I think you should know that your cousin, the Dowager Lady Bletchley, died last night."

"Send a wreath," the Marquis said automatically as he was signing the letters which his secretary had handed to him.

"Of course, My Lord. The Funeral is to take place in the country, as Her Ladyship died at her son's house."

The Marquis raised his head.

"Am I mistaken in thinking that Her Ladyship had a house in London near here?"

"Indeed she had, My Lord. In South Street, to be precise. Number Nineteen, you will recall, looks different from the other houses."

The Marquis looked at his secretary, and as the eyes of the two men met, Mr. Ashworth gave an exclamation.

"It is certainly a possibility, My Lord!"

"I think I am right in saying that Her Ladyship has not been in residence there this past year."

"I would not know the answer to that, My Lord."

"I remember hearing," the Marquis remarked, "that she left for the country because she was ill and her eldest son arranged for her to stay in the family house."

Mr. Ashworth was silent, knowing that the Marquis was thinking out loud rather than trying to have a conversation.

"I am also certain," he went on, "that she will leave her house in Mayfair to her second son, a young man who has quite a propensity for gambling. I have often seen him at White's. If I go there at once, I may find him before he leaves for the country."

"The Funeral is not until the day after tomorrow, My Lord."

"Then undoubtedly Charlie Bletchley will be at White's," the Marquis said, rising to his feet.

As he hurried from the room, almost running in his eagerness, Mr. Ashworth stared after him in astonishment.

What had happened? What could have caused this sudden outburst of energy?

It was something, he decided, which had also swept away the indolent, often cynical manner with which the Marquis regarded the world—a which which Mr. Ashworth had often deprecated in so young a man.

There was certainly nothing cynical about the Marquis now as he drove towards Islington.

Lady Bletchley's house was everything he wanted for Cyrilla.

Of course the whole place would have to be redecorated from top to bottom, but Her Ladyship had inherited from her side of the family some very attractive furniture which, the Marquis thought, would certainly be acceptable until he could find better pieces to replace them.

The house itself had been built in the last century by Robert Adam and had the attraction of large, airy rooms, fine cornices, exquisite fireplaces, and parquet floors.

The curtains and carpets, while not good enough for what the Marquis required, were unobtrusive but in excellent taste, and he thought that after the property and privation of Islington, Cyrilla would be overjoyed with her new home.

There was a small but attractive garden which had been well kept and was now filled with tulips and daffodils and several fruit-trees which were just coming into blossom.

As the Marquis stood looking at them he felt he could almost see them framing and enhancing Cyrilla's dream-like loveliness, and he felt a sudden, violent urge to be with her, to hold her in his arms, and most of all to kiss her lips.

The Marquis had kissed many women in his life, but he knew that never had he known such enchantment, such an indescribable rapture, as he felt when he kissed Cyrilla and knew that she was feeling as he did.

"I love her!" he told himself. "I had not the slightest conception that I could ever feel like this and discover it was love."

He wanted to laugh at the intensity of his feelings—then he knew that it was impossible to feel anything but grateful that he had found perfection in love, just as he had found it in Art and in sport.

He was fortunate in finding Charlie Bletchley

only too willing to sell for a very generous sum the house he had inherited from his mother.

As the Marquis had anticipated, Charlie's debts were astronomical and there was little chance of his repaying them except from what he had hoped to inherit.

The Marquis did not stay long at White's, and when he left he had bought the house in South Street with its contents and had obtained the previous owner's permission to move in without waiting for the bills-of-sale to be signed formally.

"I must say, you do not waste much time, Cousin Virgol" Charlie Bletchley said. "I expected to have this house on my hands for several months before I found a buyer, and that meant I would have to pay caretakers and Heaven knows what else!"

"It was obviously fate that everything should happen as it has," the Marquis replied lightly.

As he drove away from White's he was thinking that fate was certainly on his side.

It was fate that had made Frans Wyntack offer his second fake to Isaacs, who undoubtedly was under the influence of fate when he had taken it to the Prince of Wales.

'I suppose I shall have to tell him one day that the picture is not what it purports to be,' the Marquis thought, but he knew this was something he would not mention at the moment, for fear that the Prince would learn about Cyrilla.

"She is mine, only mine!" the Marquis told himself.

He felt a thrill as he thought how exciting it would be to enter the house in South Street and know that once they had shut the door, they would be alone and no-one could intrude upon them.

He went to bed late, for there were so many things he had to think about and plan, but he rose early as usual.

He would have left for Islington as soon as he had

returned from his ride in the Park if Mr. Ashworth has not been waiting for him.

The Surveyor who had been looking over the house on his instructions had found certain short-comings which had to be seen to at once.

Although on other occasions the Marquis might have left it entirely to his secretary, where Cyrilla was concerned he felt that nothing was too small to warrant his own personal attention.

He also found it easier to inspect in person what had to be done before giving orders.

He therefore went with the Surveyor and his secretary to the house in South Street and while he was there he found innumerable other details on which he needed to exercise his authority.

However, he went up the stairs alone to a large bedroom with a bow-window overlooking the garden.

It had a bed with an exquisitely carved and gilded head-board of mermaids and dolphins. It also had a quilted satin cover of Nile blue, which he knew was a colour which would be perfect with Cyrilla's strangely beautiful hair.

He stood for a moment imagining her in the bed, knowing that because it was so big she would look very small and ethereal with that delicate dreamy quality which Lochner had portrayed so accurately.

"I love her and I will make her happy," the Marquis swore to himself.

At the same time, just for a moment he almost felt as if the ghosts of all the other women to whom he had made love stood between him and the purity and innocence of Cyrilla.

Then as if he forced the thought away from him, he walked to the window to stand looking out into the garden.

He had the strange feeling that Cyrilla was like a snow-drop, beautiful and delicate when it grew in the ground under the shade of the trees but which never seemed the same when one picked it.

He wondered if making love to Cyrilla would spoil something flower-like and vulnerable about her, something which was so pure and holy that perhaps it should remain a spiritual aspiration just out of reach.

Then he told himself that their love would not be spoilt but would become more intense, more ecstatic, because she would be a part of him and therefore human.

"I worship her!" he told himself. "I will never do anything to hurt her in any way."

With all the details to be settled, it was getting on for noon when finally he set out for Islington.

He thought Cyrilla might be anxious, but he knew she would understand when he told her that she could leave immediately.

He had instructed Mr. Ashworth to send a closed carriage for Hannah and the luggage, having decided that Cyrilla would drive with him in his Phaeton because he knew that she would appreciate his team of magnificent chestnuts which were unequalled in the whole of London.

His horses carried him so swiftly to Islington that he realised he would reach Queen Anne Terrace sooner than he had planned and it would be quite a time before the closed carriage caught up with him.

When they arrived, the groom ran to the head of the leading horse and the Marquis stepped down to strike what was almost a tattoo with the brass knocker on the unpainted door of number 17.

"She will know who is knocking," he told himself with a smile.

He looked up at the window, half-expecting to see Cyrilla peeping out at him.

He listened for footsteps in the passage but there was only silence, and after a while he knocked again, this time so loudly that several passers-by turned round in surprise at the noise he was making.

'She must be expecting me,' he thought.

He was sure that she would not be annoyed or sulking as another woman might have been.

There was still no answer, and now there was a frown between the Marquis's eyes.

It seemed strange that both Cyrilla and Hannah should have gone out shopping when they were well aware that he had said he would be back first thing in the morning.

He knocked again, then walked up and down the pavement outside the house.

If they had been so inconsiderate as to go to the shops, then they could not intend to be long.

He told himself that perhaps there was nothing to eat in the house and Cyrilla had felt hungry and decided that as he was so late he would not now arrive until after luncheon.

"I gave Hannah some money," he said to himself. "She should have had the sense to get some food in without waiting until this late hour."

After he had knocked several times more, he saw his closed carriage coming down the road.

For a second he thought what excellent horse-flesh were drawing it and that their silver harness glittering in the sunshine was very impressive.

Then it annoyed him that when everything was ready to convey Cyrilla and Hannah to South Street, they were missing.

All sorts of possibilities came to his mind, until as the carriage drew up and the footman stepped down from the box, it struck him that perhaps they were ill.

He beckoned the footman to him.

"Go round to the back of the house, Henry," he said, "and see if there is a window which is conveniently open so that you can get in. If not, smash one, but do as little damage as possible."

"Yes, M'Lord," Henry replied.

He did not look too astonished at such a strange request, and the Marquis added:

"When you get inside, open the front door for me."

"Very good, M'Lord."

Henry hurried round to the back of the house, and
about two minutes later, while the Marquis waited
impatiently, he heard a tugging at the door before
Henry shouted:

"It's locked, M'Lord, but I've got the back one
open."

The Marquis made no reply. He merely walked
round the house as Henry had done and saw that
the back door was open.

There was also a smashed window-pane in the
kitchen window.

"This door was only bolted, M'Lord, but the front
one has been locked and there's no key."

"I understand," the Marquis said.

This meant, he thought, that Hannah and Cyrilla had gone out the front way and locked the door
behind them.

But why? What was happening?

He walked into the Sitting-Room hoping to find a
clue to their extraordinary behaviour.

Then he went up to the Studio, which told him
nothing.

He stared round it, looking at the finished and
unfinished canvasses and the sofa on which he had sat
and kissed Cyrilla.

The place gave him a feeling of emptiness.

Quickly, because he had no wish to stay there, he
crossed the passage and found that there were three
bedrooms, one with a double bed, which he was sure
was where Frans Wyntack had died, and there was no
doubt that the one next door was Cyrilla's.

It was very small and very simple, and yet there
were little touches which reminded him irresistibly
of her—a frilled muslin flounce on the dressing-table,
and small, inexpensive ornaments such as a child
might collect.

When he opened the wardrobe there was a faint
fragrance of flowers and he saw a few, a very few,
gowns hanging neatly in a row.

A sense or relief swept away some of his tensions.

She had certainly not left the house for long, as her clothes were still there.

Then for some reason which he could not afterwards recall, he went into the room next door.

It was small, smaller than Cyrilla's, and he knew that this must be where Hannah slept.

It was severe, almost like a nun's cell, which he felt was characteristic of her.

His instinct made him open the wardrobe.

It was empty!

The Marquis drew in his breath and opened the drawers of a chest. They were empty too!

There was not one piece of clothing or even a pair of shoes left in this room.

He stood very still; at the same time, there was an expression on his face which was frightening.

* * *

Late that night, after Cyrilla had gone to bed, Hannah had asked to see the Duke.

He was sitting in his favourite chair by the fireplace, and when he told Burton he would see her, she came slowly towards him and curtseyed.

"I understand," he said, "I have to thank you, Hannah, for bringing Lady Cyrilla back to me. I only wish you had done so sooner."

"I wanted to do so, Your Grace."

"I understand," the Duke said. "At the same time, now that she is home with me I want everything forgotten; the past eight years are to be wiped out completely. They are not to be talked about to anyone in the household, nor to Her Ladyship. Do you understand?"

"I understand, Your Grace."

"I am grateful to you, Hannah, for your care of my daughter. I hope you will continue to give her the same devoted attention in the future as you have done in the past."

"I'll do my best, Your Grace."

The Duke waited, aware that Hannah had something more to say.

"There's just one thing, Your Grace."

"What is it?"

"I'm going back to the house first thing in the morning to fetch my own clothes. I'm thankful there'll be no need to fetch Lady Cyrilla's. What I want to know is, what does Your Grace want done about the house?"

As if she felt that the Duke did not understand, Hannah explained:

"It belongs to Her Ladyship now and I have the deeds in my keeping."

The Duke thought for a moment, then said:

"Burn them, and let the house fall to the ground!"

"Fall to the ground, Your Grace?"

"It will make a suitable funeral-pyre, Hannah, and we will not speak of it again."

Hannah drew in her breath.

"Very good, Your Grace."

She had hurried to Islington while Cyrilla was still asleep and returned within the hour.

She had packed her own clothes but nothing of Cyrilla's, and only when she reached the top of the stairs had she hesitated outside the Studio.

Then she had gone in and taken from the drawer where Cyrilla had replaced it the sketch done by Frans Wyntack of her mother.

When Hannah held it in her hands and looked down at the loveliness of the Duchess's face, her eyes had softened.

Then as if she was afraid she might cry, she had slipped the picture into a bag she carried and hurried down the stairs.

Almost as if he was told to do so by some inner voice, the Marquis paused at exactly the same place.

He left Hannah's bedroom and walked again into the Studio, crossing the room to look in the drawer where he remembered Cyrilla had placed the sketch of her mother when she had given him the one of herself.

It was not there!

He then pulled open all the other drawers of the chest, but even as he did so he knew that he would not find the portrait—it had gone, as Cyrilla herself had.

For a moment he felt like shouting, beating his fists against the walls, overturning and breaking everything in the Studio and elsewhere in the house.

Then years of self-control made him walk down the stairs and out through the back door to his Phaeton.

He climbed into it and started to drive down the Terrace even though he felt it was almost impossible to behave in a normal and outwardly correct manner and not display his frustrations and anger very differently.

It could not be true! She could not really have gone! he told himself over and over again.

Because he could still not believe it, when he had driven halfway towards Mayfair he turned his horses and went back to Islington.

He had left the back door on the latch and it was easy to enter the house again. Now, more than he had done at first, he felt the chill of emptiness as if the very spirit of the house had departed and left only a shell.

Because he could not help himself, he went up the stairs and into Cyrilla's bedroom.

Here at least there was a fragrance of her and he felt too as if her ghost were waiting there for him.

"How could you do this to me, my darling?" he asked. "How could you leave me after all we said to each other?"

Then because he could not believe it, he told himself that there was an explanation: she must have had an accident and been taken to Hospital.

Hannah would be with her.

Knowing Cyrilla, he felt she could not deliberately have walked out of his life, could not have intentionally made him suffer as he was beginning to do.

It would be impossible for her to be so cruel.

He left the house and this time he actually reached Berkeley Square, aware that every yard he drove made him more depressed, made the fear that rising within him seem like a serpent which would poison him.

It was a fear that threatened to sap even his mind so that he could not think clearly.

If Cyrilla had gone, what could he do about it? Where could he find her? Where could he even begin to search?

Then as he stepped out of his Phaeton and went into his house, he told himself that there must be some logical explanation.

"Luncheon is ready, M'Lord," the Butler said calmly as if he was not aware of the Marquis's disturbed expression.

The Marquis told himself that when luncheon was over he would return to Islington and find Cyrilla waiting for him.

'She must have misunderstood what I told her,' he thought reassuringly; but the emptiness he had found in Hannah's bedroom was there to haunt him.

But if Hannah's clothes had gone, why had not Cyrilla's?

The Marquis went through the motions of having luncheon, but he had no idea what he ate or drank.

His secretary asked to see him when the meal was finished, but he refused, knowing that Mr. Ashworth was going to talk about the house. He could not bear for the moment to speak of it because of his growing fear that he would never be able to find the person for whom it was intended.

He went back to Islington and stayed there, regardless of the fact that his horses were fidgeting outside, for over two hours.

He sat in the little Sitting-Room where Cyrilla had first run into his arms for comfort and protection after Frans Wyntack had died, and he thought over everything that had happened since the moment he had found her and everything they had said to each other.

For the first time it struck him that she had behaved strangely, although he had not thought so at the time, when he had spoken of the house he would buy for her, where they would be together.

"I do not ... think I understand ... about the ... house."

He could almost hear her soft voice now, hesitating and stammering over the words.

"It will be yours," he had replied. "I shall give it to you and the deeds will be in your name. Whatever happens in the future, you will have somewhere to live and enough money to keep you in comfort."

He remembered how he had pulled her against · him and had gone on to say:

"You are mine, my little 'Virgin of the Lilies,' and I will look after you, protect you, and keep you from anxiety for the rest of your life. That I swear, and, my darling, we will be happier than any two people have ever been since the beginning of time."

He remembered that as he had finished speaking she had not said anything because he had kissed her until the feelings she aroused in him were unlike anything he had ever known before in his whole life.

Her lips had brought him an ecstasy that it would have been impossible to put into words, impossible to describe, and he could only recall that it had been an effort of sheer will-power to take his lips from hers and rise to his feet.

He had told her that he must leave because there were so many things for him to do, and he had said:

"I had difficulty in finding you, difficulty in getting into the house first with you and then with Hannah trying to keep me out. Now I feel I am invincible because you love me and I love you!"

Because it had been impossible not to do so, he had pulled her to her feet and kissed her soft lips once again.

He had never known a woman's lips could be so sweet, so tender, and yet have an irresistible magic about them.

It was with a tremendous effort that he had forced himself to leave her and go down the stairs, feeling he was leaving behind everything that had ever mattered to him in his life.

Now, looking back, he realised that she had not spoken.

She had not said she was pleased about the house. She had not made any reply or comment on his plans.

What had been wrong? What could have worried her? the Marquis questioned.

Then suddenly, almost as if a voice said it for him, he understood—she wanted to marry him!

It had never struck the Marquis for one moment that Cyrilla should be his wife.

This was understandable because always he had known that the woman he married would be in an entirely different category from the women who attracted him and to whom he made love.

Vaguely, because he knew it was inevitable since someday he must have an heir, he had known that he must marry, but he did not intend to do so until he was actually obliged to because of impending old age, which was something that was still far away from him.

His wife, he imagined, would be beautiful and sophisticated, a woman who would grace the end of his table, entertain with the same charm and efficiency as his mother had done, and receive the Prince of Wales and any other Royalty they asked to their house with the same self-assurance that he himself had.

As the Marchioness of Fane his wife would be very social, invited to every Ball, every Assembly, and every Reception that took place in the *Beau Monde*.

She would, of course, accompany him always to Carlton House, where, because of his long friendship with His Royal Highness, undoubtedly she would also be a favourite of the Prince.

How could he have imagined even for one second, he asked himself, that Cyrilla, with her exquisite, unworldly beauty, her strange spiritual loveliness, would fit into that category?

He could hardly believe that she would expect to do so, and yet when he thought about it, he supposed women who were pure would think love-making a sin unless they had the blessing of the Church.

The Marquis was so used to his own raffish life that he had never for one moment considered that in the eyes of what he called "good women," he was a wicked philanderer who sinned in the sight of God.

That was very different from being a rake, from having what the Prince called a "bad reputation with the fair sex," and from incurring the displeasure and condemnation of the older generation simply because the women who loved him behaved, like Lady Isabel Chatley, in an emotional and exaggerated manner.

He quite expected to be censured for that sort of behaviour, and when he thought it over, he was certain that this was not what Cyrilla was feeling but something very different.

To her love was holy, sacred! He remembered how she had said in her entrancing, hesitating little voice:

"How can I ever be . . . grateful enough to God for . . . sending you to me?"

That was what he had been—a Knight in shining armour, guided to her by a Divine Power to save her from her loneliness and fear.

Slowly, the Marquis spelt it all out to himself.

Cyrilla was different from any other woman he had known. She was young and innocent, and her ideals were unspoilt, untouched by worldly values.

It would never have struck her when they had first kissed and they said they loved each other that the Marquis did not intend that they should be married, should be man and wife.

"How could I not have realised that?" he asked

himself. "Then I could have explained everything to her."

But what could he have explained? That she was not important enough socially to be his wife? That her blood was not as blue as his? That her parents did not bear the scrutiny of those who thought a Family Tree more important than love?

How could he have said any of those things? And yet, how else could he explain that he could not marry her?

Even as he asked himself the question he knew it was an absurd one.

Of course he was prepared to marry Cyrilla, if that was what she wanted. He would certainly marry her rather than lose her, and if that was what he had done, it was entirely his own fault.

Yet, how could he have known? How could he have guessed? he questioned despairingly.

He felt that his cry echoed round and round the small room and came back again, meaningless, to his ears.

Then another question came to his mind: Why had her mother's tombstone been worded so strangely?

Could it possibly be that she had not been Frans Wyntack's wife, as he had naturally assumed she was? If her mother had not been married, that would account, perhaps, for Cyrilla's reluctance to enter into the same sort of liaison.

In fact, it could have given her a horror of anything irregular and unconventional.

"Why did she not tell me?" the Marquis asked aloud. "If she had only trusted me!"

He could see the tombstone clearly:

Lorraine
Beloved of Frans Wyntack and Cyrilla

Now he was sure that Cyrilla, although she had called him "Papa," was not really Frans Wyntack's daughter; but how could that fact help him find her?

Once again he went to Cyrilla's bedroom.

'Come back to me!' he called in his heart, and stood there feeling that somehow, because he could sense her so vividly, she must hear what he was saying.

'Come back to me! Let me explain! Let me tell you that my love for you is great enough for anything —even marriage!'

Just for a moment he questioned if that was true. Then as if a barrier within him fell, he knew that it was.

He wanted Cyrilla, wanted her with him for the rest of his life. She was his, she was a part of him. He could no more lose her than lose one of his limbs.

His whole being cried out for her. He felt as if he were drowning in an ocean of despair and frustration and only she could save him.

Then he had the terrifying conviction that he had in fact lost her forever.

* * *

As the dressmaker curtseyed and went from Cyrilla's bedroom, Hannah put over her shoulders the robe of satin and lace which they had just brought.

Cyrilla walked to the window to stand looking out on the trees in the Park.

Every time she did so, she thought of the garden the Marquis had described to her.

She could almost see him coming towards her through the flowers.

"You look tired," Hannah said, behind her.

Cyrilla wanted to reply that she was unhappy, but she knew there was no point in saying so.

"A little," she admitted, "but then I am not used to trying on so many clothes all at once!"

"You'll do them credit," Hannah said. "The gownmaker said as she went down the stairs: 'There's no beauty in the whole of London Society who can hold a candle to Her Ladyship.'"

"I am not . . . going into . . . Society," Cyrilla said quickly in a frightened voice. "Papa promised me!"

"No! We're going to the country the day after tomorrow," Hannah said soothingly. "His Grace told me so today. I want you to meet people of your own age and to make friends."

"I shall be quite content as I am with Papa," Cyrilla replied.

"That's foolish and you know it!" Hannah said in her usual sharp manner. "But it's early days to worry, and when you get back to the Castle you'll feel different."

"Perhaps."

Cyrilla sighed, still staring out the window; and after a moment, as if she could not restrain her curiosity, Hannah asked:

"What are you thinking about?"

"I am . . . thinking of the . . . empty house and . . . the Marquis. . . ."

"Forget it!" Hannah said. "Forget him. You have to try. It'll be hard—I know that. But after all, you only knew him for a short time."

"I do not think . . . time has any bearing on one's feelings," Cyrilla said dreamily. "Love just . . . happens. He was there . . . and it would have been exactly the . . . same if it had taken . . . years instead of minutes."

"That sort of thinking's not going to help!" Hannah snapped.

"I was just . . . wondering," Cyrilla said, "if . . . anything will help. I feel as if I have lost part of myself. Something has . . . gone, and I think it is my . . . heart."

Hannah made an irritated sound which told Cyrilla that she was annoyed.

As if she had nothing more to say, she moved about the room rather noisily, opening and closing drawers, moving a chair.

When Cyrilla did not speak, she said coaxingly:

"Come and put on one of your new gowns. His

Grace'll be wanting you to pour out tea for him, and he'll want to see you in your finery."

It flashed through Cyrilla's mind that the person for whom she wanted to model her new gowns was not her father, but she did not say so.

Instead she allowed Hannah to dress her in an attractive gown which had been extremely expensive and which made her look like the goddess of the dawn.

Hannah noticed that she hardly bothered to glance at herself in the mirror, and when she was ready, she went downstairs with an expression on her face which made the old Nurse draw in her breath.

"That man! Why did he have to come into her life at just the wrong moment?" she asked herself. "Only a few days later and she'd have been here and not even aware that anyone called the Marquis of Fane existed. Why, why did it have to happen?"

It was a cry that human beings had made since the beginning of time, railing against fate, knowing they could do nothing about it.

Cyrilla was thinking the same thing.

It would have been very exciting to be at home with Papa. Exciting to know that she was going to the Castle. Exciting to realise that in a few months' time she would see her brother again. If . . .

If! That was the snag! If only she had not met the Marquis. If only she had not fallen in love. If only she did not feel her whole body crying out for him.

"I love him!"

It was difficult to hear anything that was said because for her there was only the sound of his voice. It was difficult to see her surroundings because in front of her was always his face.

And every minute she felt herself recalling the wonder of his lips on hers and how in the closeness of his arms she had felt his heart beating.

* * *

The Marquis came back from Islington for the third time with a scowl on his face which made the footmen in the Hall at Fane House look at him apprehensively.

Mr. Ashworth was more courageous.

"Has something gone wrong, My Lord?"

For a moment the Marquis hesitated. Then as if he could not prevent himself, he asked:

"How do you find somebody who has disappeared? Where does one begin to search for one woman in the whole of London?"

Mr. Ashworth was not only alert but sympathetic. Now he understood what had happened.

"You have lost the lady for whom you bought the house, My Lord?"

"She has disappeared, Ashworth. I told her I would call for her at her house in Islington, but when I got there—and I have been there three times today—it was empty."

"Surely, My Lord . . ."

"You mean, there must be a reason, Ashworth. There was a misunderstanding between us, although I did not realise it at the time. I have to find her, do you understand? I *have* to find her!"

There was something very positive in the Marquis's assertion. At the same time, his secretary had the feeling that it was also a cry for help.

"You do not think, My Lord," Mr. Ashworth said after a moment, "that there has been an accident?"

"I thought of that," the Marquis said, "but for reasons I need not go into, I am sure that she has left the house not by chance but by intention."

"In which case, My Lord, she will be hiding from you."

"That is what I am afraid of, Ashworth. But where? In God's name, where could she go?"

"Your Lordship has no idea of anywhere she had been previously?"

"No," the Marquis replied. "And she has very little money."

Mr. Ashworth's eyes showed his surprise.

If the woman in question had no money, it

meant that the Marquis had not given her any. That was very different from his usual procedure, for he was exceedingly generous, almost absurdly so in some cases, Mr. Ashworth thought.

His suspicion was now growing stronger that the lady for whom they had bought the house was different from those whom the Marquis had known before.

His whole attitude about her was certainly strange and unlike anything Mr. Ashworth could remember in the past.

He had, of course, procured houses for a number of women who had come under the Marquis's protection, but he had certainly never expended as much on them as he had paid for Lady Bletchley's house.

In no instance that Mr. Ashworth could remember had the Marquis taken so much personal interest in supervising the details in the house itself.

Usually he had left everything to his secretary and the lady in question, insisting merely that if he was to dine there, a stock of the claret and the champagne he fancied should be delivered before he did so.

'This is different,' Mr. Ashworth thought to himself. 'His Lordship is certainly hard-hit.'

"I am wondering whether I should employ a Bow Street Runner," the Marquis said at length.

"I should think it might be a good idea, My Lord."

"I would not wish to frighten her by employing such a man, but otherwise I have no idea where to start looking."

He put out his hand in a helpless gesture as he said:

"There must be thousands of Lodging-Houses and small Hotels in London. How can I search them all? How can I even begin to guess where two women would hide so that I would not be able to find them?"

This was plain speaking and Mr. Ashworth hesitated a moment before he said:

"You do not think, My Lord, that the lady might

change her mind and perhaps send you a letter or a message so that you can contact her and make up your differences?"

He could not help feeling that if the woman whom the Marquis fancied had done anything so drastic as to run away from him, she would soon regret having been so impetuous and would make every effort to be back in the Marquis's arms again.

To Mr. Ashworth's surprise, the Marquis shook his head.

"I do not think she will change her mind," he said, and there was a note in his voice which surprised his secretary more than anything that had happened so far.

"I am going to suggest, My Lord," he said after an uncomfortable silence, "that you let me send for a Bow Street Runner. I happen to know of one who is extremely astute and at the same time discreet. He is employed from time to time by the very best people, and I know that anything you say to him would be held completely in confidence."

"Then I suppose you had better send for him," the Marquis said, as if he thought the idea was a forlorn hope.

"May I remind Your Lordship that you are dining at Carlton House this evening?" Mr. Ashworth went on. "It was arranged a week ago, and as you did not tell me to cancel the engagement, as I expected you would do this morning, I have actually done nothing."

"I had forgotten," the Marquis said.

As he spoke, he thought that he had no wish to go to Carlton House and would make some excuse.

Then he remembered that if he went there he could see the Lochner painting of Cyrilla.

He also remembered at the same time that he had the Prince's permission to take away the Van Dyck.

He had meant to send a carriage for it the next day, but then he had found Cyrilla, and she had not only put the idea out of his mind, but there had seemed no point in having a painted image of what he could see, touch, and kiss.

"I will go to Carlton House."

He rose from his chair as he spoke, adding:

"I want to see the Bow Street Runner first thing in the morning, immediately after breakfast."

"Very good, My Lord. I will do my best to see that he is here."

"God knows what else we can do," the Marquis added as he left the room.

As he walked up the stairs he was thinking that he had imagined tonight he would dine with Cyrilla in their own house together.

Afterwards he would make love to her, and it would be the most perfect and wonderful thing he had ever done in his life.

Now he was back where he had started, having only a painted face to look at and the feeling, which he knew would intensify, that although he had thought he had found her, it had only been a dream, a figment of his imagination, and she had in fact been dead for more than three hundred years.

'Cyrilla! Cyrilla!' he called in his heart.

As he entered his bedroom he saw standing on the mantelpiece the sketch of her which had been done by Frans Wyntack and which sht had given him as a present.

It was not as fine as the exquisite painting by Lochner, but it was Cyrilla with her eyes looking into another world, her hair haloed with light, her lips parted as if in sudden ecstasy.

The Marquis stared at it for a long time, then he said:

"If it takes me my whole life I will find you again. That I swear! Then nobody and nothing shall stop me from making you mine, my wife!"

Chapter Six

The Phaeton lurched and the Marquis said irritably:

"These roads are appalling!"

"It is always the same when one gets far off the highways," the Prince replied. "They would be much worse if it were wet."

The Marquis looked up at the sky.

"It looks as if that is a distinct possibility, Sire," he said pessimistically. "Those are obviously rain-clouds."

The Prince did not reply. He knew that the Marquis was depressed and had made no effort to hide his boredom ever since they had left London.

His Royal Highness was almost regretting that he had done what he thought was a Samaritan's act in forcing the Marquis to come with him to the country.

"You have refused every invitation I have offered you, Virgo, for the last month," he had said, "and from all I hear, you spend your time riding round the back-streets of London, with God knows what object."

He paused for the Marquis's reply, but as there was none, he went on:

"You have lost weight and if you are not careful you will lose your looks."

As the Prince spoke, he thought this was very unlikely.

But the Marquis was in fact very much thinner

and there was a hollow look about his eyes, as if he had not been sleeping.

The Prince was bewildered, as were all the Marquis's other friends, but now he was determined to get to the bottom of what they were all describing as "Fane's strange behaviour."

"I want you," he had said aloud, "to drive me down to Searle's place in Hampshire. I suppose you have heard he is selling his stable?"

"Selling his stable?" the Marquis repeated incredulously, and the Prince knew that at last he had captured his friend's attention.

"Gambling-debts," he explained before the Marquis could ask the question. "He has been selling everything else for the last year and now his horses have to go."

The Marquis certainly found it inconceivable, because the Earl of Searle's horse-flesh was outstanding and he had won several important races which would have brought in good prize-money.

"What I am determined," the Prince went on, "and I am sure you are, too, is to get the pick of the sale before we are out-bid, and Searle has agreed that we should be the first to look over the horses."

"That was certainly a very astute move on your part, Sire," the Marquis remarked. "I wonder how you managed it?"

There was a faint smile on the Prince's lips before he answered:

"I am not going to tell you all my secrets, but as I consider you to be a better judge of horse-flesh than anybody else in the country, I am asking—no, commanding—you to drive me to Hampshire tomorrow."

There was nothing the Marquis could do but agree, although he admitted to himself that the idea of buying some of Searle's outstanding animals did for a moment raise his spirits a trifle from the despondency into which they had been cast for the last four weeks.

It was true, as the Prince had said, that he had

spent his days riding round the back-streets of London, praying and hoping that he would catch a glimpse of Cyrilla or Hannah.

Wherever they were living, they would have to go out sometime during the day, and they would have to go to the poorer shops. He was quite certain that by now they would be desperately in need of money.

The Bow Street Runner he had employed had visited a great number of different places where the staple foods could be bought, but although he had given a very vivid description of Hannah, no-one recalled having seen her.

When the Marquis was alone night after night in Berkeley Square, he thought sometimes he would go mad at the thought that he had lost Cyrilla through what he admitted was entirely his own stupidity.

"How could I have been such a fool," he had asked himself, "not to understand her better, not to realise that she is not like other women?"

But rebuking himself did not help to find her, and invariably the next morning he was riding again; and inevitably, because hope died hard, he found his way at least twice a day back to the little house in Islington.

He would tie up his horse and enter through the back door and look searchingly to see if he could detect whether anyone else had been there except himself.

Surely, he had thought, Cyrilla would come back for her gowns.

But they still hung there exactly as when he had first seen them, and he could have sworn that no-one had touched anything else in her bedroom.

Almost inevitably at some time of the day or night he would tell himself that he had in fact dreamt the whole episode.

Because her face as portrayed in the sketch was etched on his mind, he tried to convince himself that to believe he had found her was nothing more than an hallucination.

Then he knew that when he had touched her lips, it had been more real than any other kiss he had ever given or received, and if he lived to be a hundred he would never forget the ecstasy and the rapture he had found at that moment.

In his own misery, the Marquis had no idea how much Mr. Ashworth and the rest of his household worried about him.

Because by this time they all knew that he was searching for the beautiful girl whose portrait stood on the mantelpiece in his bedroom, they too walked about the streets, looking to see if they could find her, knowing that their Master would never be happy until someone did.

Because he was determined to be more practical in his help, instead of just gossiping as they did in White's over the Marquis's unpredictable behaviour, the Prince had been thinking for some time of an excuse to get him alone.

It had not been easy, for the Marquis had refused every invitation the Prince had given him, and it was in fact almost with an air of triumph that the Prince stepped into the Marquis's Phaeton where it was waiting for him outside Carlton House.

"The Landau with our luggage has gone ahead," he announced, "so our valets will have everybody ready for us when we arrive. I will say one thing for Searle—he has a good cellar!"

"How many horses are you thinking of buying, Sire?" the Marquis asked as they drove off.

As the Prince pondered the question, the Marquis thought slightly cynically that really the answer should be: "As many as you are prepared to give me," because he was quite certain that he would have to pay for the Prince's purchases.

He was prepared to do so. At the same time, there were, he remembered, several horses of Searle's that he would wish to own himself, and that was the only reason he was prepared to leave London and abandon for two days his search for Cyrilla.

At the beginning of this week he had engaged two more Bow Street Runners, and he had told Ashworth, before he left, that if there was any news of any sort, to send a groom post-haste to the Earl's house and he would return immediately.

"I can only hope it is something I shall have to do, My Lord," Mr. Ashworth had said.

As he spoke, he could not help thinking that it was a very unlikely contingency.

"You are right," the Prince said now. "It is going to rain. It is unfortunate that your Phaeton has no hood."

"I never bother with one," the Marquis replied. "It makes the vehicle heavier."

"Heavy or not, I have no wish to arrive looking like a drowned rat," the Prince said irritably.

The Marquis, feeling the heavy spots of rain on his face, touched his horses with the whip. Then as they responded, moving a little too fast for caution round the corner of the lane, for it was little more on which they were travelling, there appeared a farmcart driving in the centre of the road and the yokel in charge of it was half-asleep.

"Look out!" the Prince shouted unnecessarily, and the Marquis, with remarkable expertise, managed to draw his horses almost into the hedge to avoid a head-on collision. But a wheel of the Phaeton scraped against a wheel of the farm-wagon.

There was a shout from the yokel and an oath from the Prince as the Marquis drew his startled horses to a standstill.

"Wot d'ye think ye're a-doin' of?" the yokel shouted, obviously frightened out of his complacency.

"It would be better, my man, if you did not drive in the centre of the road!" the Marquis retorted.

"'Ow was Oi ter know ye were a-coming roun' t' corner loik a whirlwind?" the yokel asked.

The groom ran to the horses' heads and the Marquis stepped down from the Phaeton to inspect the damage.

As he had anticipated, the wheel was buckled, not badly but enough to require immediate attention.

"What has happened? Can we proceed?" the Prince asked.

"Where is the nearest blacksmith?" the Marquis asked the yokel.

He considered the question before he replied:

"There be one up at t' Castle."

"Which Castle?" the Marquis questioned.

The yokel pointed with a dirty finger towards some trees.

The Marquis's eyes followed the direction and he could see the top of a tower and on it was flying a standard.

"Who lives there?" he asked.

"It be 'is Grace."

"The Duke of what?" the Marquis asked.

"That be Holm Castle, where th' Duke o' Holm-bury lives," the yokel replied, "an' this be 'is cart which ye've bin a'knocking about."

The Marquis drew a guinea from his pocket and flicked it in the air, and the yokel caught it with the bemused expression of one who cannot believe his good luck.

Then as he bit the coin to see if it was real, the Marquis climbed back into the Phaeton.

"I suppose we have to go to Holm Castle," the Prince said as the horses, now held on a tight rein, proceeded very slowly.

"I doubt if there is another blacksmith within miles," the Marquis replied.

"Holm dislikes me and always has," the Prince said. "I have always known that he sided with my father in rows over my debts and that he is hand-in-glove with my mother. I can tell without asking what he thinks of me."

The Marquis gave a laugh with no humour in it.

"I am certainly not one of his favourites either. He has cut me ostentatiously ever since a short affair I had with one of his cousins. It was something I regretted because she was uncommonly boring, but I doubt if he would accept that as an excuse."

The Prince laughed.

"I can see we shall not have a warm welcome. How long will it take?"

"About two hours," the Marquis said.

The Prince looked up at the sky as he said:

"I would be prepared to sit with the devil himself rather than be outside in the rain. Let us hope the Duke will at least offer us a glass of claret."

The Marquis did not reply.

If he had been a little more intuitive, he might have been aware that not only the Prince but fate was laughing.

* * *

Cyrilla tidied away the game of chess she had been playing with her father.

"You are too good, Papa!" she said. "But I shall go on trying to beat you, and I think it is a fascinating game and requires more intelligence than any other."

"That is true," the Duke agreed; "and it has always struck me as strange that men who otherwise have a good brain should waste their time gambling on the turn of a card and believing in something called 'luck.'"

"It is ridiculous, I agree," Cyrilla said.

As she put the chess-board in the corner of the room, she wondered whether the Marquis gambled.

It seemed unlikely. At the same time, she thought how little she really knew about him except that she loved him and everything she did or thought brought him more vividly to her mind.

"I see it is raining," she said, glancing out the window. "That is disappointing, as I did want you to come and see if the new goldfish have settled down with the others."

"We shall see them tomorrow," the Duke replied,

"and instead today we will go into the Orangery. I have ordered some new orchids of which I am sure you will approve."

"Oh, Papa, how exciting!" Cyrilla said. "And the orange-trees are in blossom; I had forgotten how lovely they were."

She found there were quite a lot of things in the Castle she had forgotten, and even after she had been there a month, every day she found something new to discuss with her father.

She tried to hide from him her feeling that everything was a waste of time and that every smile she gave was an effort.

She believed that he thought she was completely happy and that Hannah was the only person who knew the truth.

"There are some more plants I intend buying for the Orangery," the Duke began, "and you must tell me—"

The door opened and Burton announced:

"His Royal Highness, the Prince of Wales!"

For a moment the Duke was so surprised that he did not rise to his feet.

Then as he did so, the Prince, looking large and flamboyant and oozing charm, as he could do most effectively when he pleased, bore down upon him.

"You must forgive this intrusion," he said, holding out his hand, "but we have had a slight accident at your very gates, which has resulted most regrettably in a bent wheel. If I may ask for your hospitality for only an hour or so, I should be extremely grateful."

The Duke bowed his head.

"Your Royal Highness is welcome to anything I can offer. I have a blacksmith here at the Castle."

"So I have already learnt," the Prince replied, "and he is at this very moment, I believe, examining the wheel."

"I hope I may offer Your Royal Highness some refreshment," the Duke said.

"Thank you, thank you!" the Prince replied, and

looked meaningfully towards Cyrilla, who was standing at her father's side.

She was thinking, in fact, that the Prince was exactly as she had imagined he would be, and she noted the twinkle in his eye which told her that he was well aware that her father was somewhat discomfited by his sudden appearance.

"May I present, Sire, my daughter, Lady Cyrilla Holm," the Duke said formally.

"Enchanted! Absolutely enchanted!" the Prince said, looking at Cyrilla with the admiring expression in his eyes with which he regarded every pretty woman.

Then as she curtseyed he exclaimed:

"Surely we have met? Or have I seen you somewhere before?"

"N-no . . . Your Royal Highness," Cyrilla replied; at the same time, the colour rose in her cheeks.

She was well aware where the Prince had seen her.

Then as the Prince began:

"But I am sure I am not mistaken. I have seen you. I never forget a face!"

"The Marquis of Fane!" Burton announced.

The Duke had been surprised at the Prince's appearance, but as Cyrilla looked towards the door she froze into immobility.

The Marquis, for the moment unaware of her presence, walked down the room, his eyes on the Duke, wondering as he came what his reluctant host would say when he learnt that it would take longer to repair the wheel than he had at first thought.

It was only as he drew nearer that he became aware that the Duke was looking at him in an extremely hostile fashion and the Prince was staring at someone standing beside him.

He took just a fleeting glance at the object of His Royal Highness's attention, then froze as Cyrilla had.

He stopped completely still and looked at her,

his eyes widening, and he knew that his whole body had come alive!

She was here! She was standing in front of him and his search was over!

"Cyrilla!"

He heard his voice say her name and was surprised that he was able to speak.

The Duke was frowning but the Prince looked from the Marquis to Cyrilla, then gave a sudden exclamation.

"Now I know who she reminds me of, and I know too who you have been looking for—the Virgin in the Lochner painting!"

The Prince's voice ringing out broke the spell which had held the Marquis motionless.

He stepped forward to Cyrilla's side, took her hand in his, and said in a voice fraught with emotion:

"I have—found you! How could you leave me? How could you be so cruel? I have been distraught— off my head—because I thought I would never find you again!"

Cyrilla looked up into his eyes and it seemed to her at that moment that the whole world had turned a somersault and fallen back into place exactly as it should be.

The Marquis was there and she was no longer alone and unhappy.

He was telling her of his love and she was giving him hers and they were together again.

Then abruptly the Duke took command of the situation.

"I understand, Fane," he said, "that you have met my daughter before and treated her in a manner which is certainly not to your credit."

With an effort the Marquis looked away from Cyrilla and faced the Duke.

He stared at him as if he did not understand what he was saying; then as if with difficulty, he found words, he said:

"I can explain, Your Grace."

"It is quite unnecessary," the Duke said sharply. "Cyrilla, will you ask Burton to bring wine for His Royal Highness? Then please retire to your own room."

"Y-yes . . . Papa!" Cyrilla replied, after a moment's hesitation.

"No! You cannot leave me!" the Marquis said, holding on to her hand.

It was as if he had come back to sanity.

She gave him a quick, frightened little glance, and, taking her hand away, moved across the room in obedience to her father's command.

Fearing for a moment that the Marquis might follow her, the Duke said quickly:

"Will Your Royal Highness sit down? And you, Fane—perhaps you would be kind enough to tell me what verdict my blacksmith has given on the condition of your wheel."

The Marquis's eyes were still following Cyrilla.

She had reached the door, and now she opened it and passed through, without looking back.

With an effort he sat down on a chair opposite the Duke, saying as he did so:

"The wheel? Oh yes, the wheel of the Phaeton! I am afraid it may take several hours."

"I hope Your Grace will not feel we are imposing on your hospitality," the Prince said.

"Of course not, Sire," the Duke replied. "And may I offer you some food, if you have not had luncheon?"

"We ate," the Prince replied, "although I could hardly call it an adequate meal, on our way here. If, before we leave, you could offer me a small repast, I assure you I should not refuse."

"It will be seen to," the Duke replied.

He looked up as the door opened.

"Ah, here is the wine. I hope it will be to your liking, knowing you are a connoisseur in this field."

He did not make it sound like a compliment and

the Prince was astute enough to know that it was not
intended to be one.

His lips twitched, but he said quite gravely:

"Your Grace is too kind. Fane and I are extremely
grateful."

Burton, with a footman carrying a silver tray,
moved towards the Prince, and the Duke made a
formal bow and went from the room.

As he reached the Hall he saw Cyrilla standing
at the bottom of the stairs, and he had the feeling that
she was trying to make up her mind whether to defy
him and return to the Salon, or to go upstairs as she
had been ordered to do.

When she saw her father she ran towards him.

"Please . . . Papa, please," she said, "I must . . ."
see the Marquis . . . alone for a . . . moment. Please . . .
let me."

The Duke shook his head.

"There is no point in your being made more
miserable than you have been already," he said.

Cyrilla looked at him sharply and he said:

"I am not blind, my dear. I know how you have
been suffering, but nothing can be solved by talking
about it. You know his feelings on the matter. Of
course they may have changed because of the difference in your circumstances, but are you really
prepared to believe any explanation he offers you?"

Her father was expressing what Cyrilla had already thought herself.

For a moment she did not speak; then she said
in a voice which was devoid of all feeling:

"I am . . . sure you are . . . right, Papa," and started
to walk up the stairs.

The Duke watched her for a moment, then sighed
and walked down the passage towards the office of the
Groom of the Chambers.

He was determined to feed and wine the Prince,
then get rid of him and the Marquis of Fane as
quickly as possible.

Meeting a footman, he sent him in search of the

Estate Manager, who he thought would be able to expedite the repair of the Phaeton's wheel quicker than anyone else.

Cyrilla was moving slowly up the stairs, as if her youth had left her and she had suddenly grown old.

She had almost reached the top step when she heard the door open below her and without really meaning to, without consciously thinking about it, she looked down.

She saw the Marquis come out of the Salon and into the Hall and hurry to the front door, where there were two footmen on duty.

"Where is Lady Cyrilla?" she heard him ask.

The footman to whom he spoke looked up towards her before he replied, and the Marquis, following his gaze, saw her too.

He came up the stairs two at a time. When he reached her he took her hand in his and led her onto the landing.

"I have to speak to you, I have to!" he said urgently. "Show me where we can talk."

The urgency in his voice communicated itself to her and she moved quickly ahead of him and opened the door which led into the Sitting-Room which was attached to the bedroom she was using.

She had made it very personal, with a painting of her mother on a small easel by the window, and if nothing else told the Marquis it belonged to her, there was a profusion of flowers everywhere.

He came into the room, shut the door behind him, and said:

"My darling! My sweet! I have found you when I thought I had lost you forever!"

There was a note in his voice which she had never heard and it drew her as nothing had ever done before.

She looked into his eyes and was lost.

The next moment his arms were round her and he was kissing her frantically, passionately, desperately, as if he had come back from the grave when he had never expected to find himself alive.

It was impossible to think; he knew only that, having been so miserable, so lost in an utter slough of despondency, he was now carrying her away into the divine light that she had known when he had kissed her the first time.

It was so perfect, so wonderful, that she could only feel as if he had given her back her heart and it was beating frantically and tumultuously against his and they were one and no-one could ever divide them again.

"I love you!" Cyrilla wanted to say, but the Marquis said it for her.

"I love you! I worship you!" he said. "How soon will you marry me?"

They were the words she had wanted him to say, and yet somehow, now that he had said them, they did not matter.

He loved her as she loved him, and it flashed through her mind that even being married could not make them closer than they were at this moment.

Then the Marquis was kissing her again, kissing her eyes, her cheeks, her chin, even her little straight nose, before he made her lips captive.

"My darling, my precious! My little love, my 'Virgin of the Lilies'! You are mine! Completely and utterly mine!"

His words were almost incoherent; then he raised his head to say:

"I have ridden all over London looking for you, so that now I know every hole and corner, every street and lane, every filthy alleyway, and you were here, here all the time, where fate has been kind enough to bring me."

"It is always . . . fate where we are . . . concerned," Cyrilla managed to whisper.

"I will never lose you again," the Marquis said. "We will be married at once. I have already procured a Special Licence to use as soon as I found you. And,

my darling, until my ring is on your finger, I swear
I will not let you out of my sight!"

He knew by the radiance in her face that this was
what she wanted.

"There are so many explanations to make to
you," he said, "so many excuses, but they are unimportant. All that really matters is that I love you and we
will be married and happy as we knew we would be
the first moment we saw each other."

"I ... love you!" Cyrilla whispered. "But ... what
will ... Papa say?"

The words came to her lips without her really
thinking about them, and even as she spoke the door
opened and the Duke came into the room.

One glance at his face told Cyrilla how angry he
was, and instinctively she moved a little nearer to the
Marquis, as if for protection.

"Your behaviour. Fane, does not surprise me!"
the Duke said scathingly. "It is what I might have
expected."

"You do not undestand, Your Grace," the Marquis replied. "May I have your permission to marry
Cyrilla? We love each other, and marriage is what we
both want."

"Marriage?" the Duke said. "So that is what you
are offering her now! You were not prepared to
offer her marriage before you were aware that she
was my daughter."

The Marquis took his arms from Cyrilla and
straightened his back.

"It is difficult to explain, Your Grace," he said,
"although I will try to do so. I do not know what
Cyrilla has told you about our meeting. but we had
no time to explain to each other anything about ourselves except that we were in love."

He saw the sneer on the Duke's face and knew
that he did not understand.

"I promise Your Grace, this is the truth. It was only after Cyrilla had run away from me that I realised
—and I admit it was extremely stupid of me—that I

should have understood that she would wish to marry me, as I wished to marry her as soon as I thought about it."

Even as he spoke, the Marquis knew he was explaining himself very badly.

"That is very easy to say now," the Duke remarked. "The fact remains, Fane, that you did not offer my daughter marriage, and let me say firmly and categorically that I am not prepared to accept you as a son-in-law."

Cyrilla gave a little cry.

"Oh, Papa! You cannot . . . mean . . . that!"

"I do mean it," the Duke said, "and both you and the Marquis will appreciate that you cannot marry now or at any time in the future without my permission, and I will not give in any circumstances."

He spoke slowly, as if he wished them to take in the full meaning of the words.

"If Your Grace will give me a chance to explain—" the Marquis began.

"Explanations are unnecessary," the Duke interrupted. "I disapprove of you, Fane, and I always have. What you call love will not alter my opinion. A leopard cannot change its spots, however hard it tries."

"But that is not . . . fair, Papa!" Cyrilla argued.

"Fair or not," the Duke replied, "you are my daughter and it is for me to decide whom you will marry and whom you will not marry."

He saw the pain in Cyrilla's expression, and he said a little more kindly:

"You have seen for the last eight years what happens when a woman goes against the conventions and defies Society. The Marquis of Fane has flouted the conventions in somewhat the same manner. I can assure you that he would not make you happy, nor would I allow you to live his type of life as his wife or as his mistress."

He looked toward the Marquis.

"I have no more to say on the matter, and I request you, My Lord, to leave my house. Doubtless you can find shelter in the stables until the wheel of your Phaeton is mended, which is being done as swiftly as possible. As soon as it is ready, you can collect His Royal Highness at the front door."

Any other time the Marquis would have refused to accept the insult, but he could only look despairingly at Cyrilla.

"I can only say," he said in a low voice, "that I love you and will go on loving you until I die."

Tears flooded Cyrilla's eyes and she could not answer him but could only clasp her hands together as the Marquis, with a dignity that was inescapable, turned towards the door and left the room without looking back.

After a moment the Duke followed him.

Slowly the tears which blinded her began to fall down Cyrilla's cheeks.

She did not sob, did not even, as she wanted to do, collapse on the ground; she only told herself that she had no wish to go on living.

* * *

It had stopped raining by the time the wheel was repaired and the Marquis drove his Phaeton round to the front door.

A message had already been sent to the Prince, who came down the steps escorted by the Duke.

"I must thank Your Grace for an excellent repast," he said, "and I hope one day I shall have the chance to repay your hospitality."

The Duke bowed in acknowledgement, and watched as the Prince was helped by two footmen into the high seat of the Phaeton beside the Marquis.

They drove off, the Marquis staring ahead and making no effort to raise his hat as the Prince did.

They had gone only a very short distance before the Prince asked:

"What the hell happened? You never came back to the Salon, and the Duke informed me that you were waiting outside."

"As he ordered me to do," the Marquis replied. "If you want to know the truth, Sire, he threw me out of the house!"

"For making love to his daughter? I do not blame you—she is even more beautiful than my painting of her."

The Marquis did not reply, and the Prince went on:

"We know now it is a fake, but a damned good one! So good, in fact, that I feel it was almost worth the money I paid for it."

He stopped, smiled, and added as if his honesty was forced from him:

"Or rather—what you paid!"

"The painting is of no importance," the Marquis said.

"But the girl is," the Prince added. "What are you going to do about her?"

"What can I do? The Duke will not give his permission for her to marry me."

The Prince's eye-brows went up.

"Caught at last, Virgo? Well, that certainly is a surprise! At the same time, I can understand. She is lovely—absolutely lovely!"

"What am I to do?" the Marquis asked.

The question seemed to be wrung from his lips.

"Run away with her?" the Prince suggested.

"I doubt if she will do that," the Marquis said. "I have only just begun to understand why she was living as she was in that squalid little house in Islington."

"Was that where you found her?" the Prince enquired. "Why should she have been doing that?"

"I remember, long ago," the Marquis said, "being told that the Duchess had left the Duke and was living in Ireland."

"You mean that instead Her Grace was living in Islington?" the Prince questioned.

"With the artist with whom she had run away," the Marquis replied.

The Prince, for all his faults, had always been quick-witted.

"Of course!" he exclaimed. "And he painted the fake of Lochner, using that lovely girl as his model. What a story! It is like something out of a novel!"

"I can only ask Your Highness, for Cyrilla's sake, not to repeat it," the Marquis begged, "and of course for—mine."

"It is the sort of story I would enjoy telling," the Prince said. "At the same time, if you ask me to keep silent, I will."

"I am asking you to help me, Sire. Cyrilla is the only woman I have ever wanted to marry. If the Duke refuses his permission, what can I do?"

The Prince thought for a moment.

"To be honest, there is very little, Virgo. You know as well as I do that if you abduct his daughter when she is under-age, you can, if he chooses to be unpleasant about it, be transported. Everyone knows your reputation with a pistol, and it is unlikely that at his age he will challenge you to a duel."

"That is what I thought," the Marquis murmured. "Do you think Lady Cyrilla will be able to change her father's mind?"

"I doubt it. I did not have the time to explain to her why I behaved as I did."

"You seem to have got yourself into a hell of a mess," the Prince remarked. "But there must be something you can do. God knows, she is beautiful enough to turn any man's head, even yours!"

"She has!" the Marquis agreed briefly.

They drove on and only when Lord Searle's house was in sight did the Marquis say, as if he was making up his mind.

"I have something to suggest to you, Sire. I hope you will understand."

"What is it?" the Prince asked.

"I do not intend to return to London tomorrow after we have seen Searle's horses."

The Prince turned to look at him in surprise.

"Then what will you do?"

"Stay near the Castle," the Marquis replied. "I have to see Cyrilla somehow, and I may be able to bribe a servant to take her a note, or perhaps find a chance to speak to her when she is riding. All I know is that having found her, I do not intend to lose her again."

He drew in his breath and added:

"Whether she wants me or not, whatever the obstacles in our way, somehow I will see her. So, whatever happens, I will be there."

* * *

"I don't know what to do about Lady Cyrilla, and that's a fact, Your Grace!" Hannah said in her downright manner.

"I have noticed that she is eating very little," the Duke answered.

"Little!" Hannah snorted. "Does Your Grace realize that I have to take in her gowns an inch or so round the waist practically every other day! And it's not right that she should be crying every night until her pillow's wet even in the morning."

The Duke walked across the Library floor and back again before he said:

"You can hardly expect me, Hannah, to countenance the Marquis of Fane, considering his behaviour towards Lady Cyrilla when he was unaware that she was my daughter."

"He was very kind, Your Grace, about the Funeral, and if any gentleman was in love, it was him. But love's one thing, as Your Grace knows, and marriage another!"

"He is not a fit and proper person to marry any young girl, least of all Lady Cyrilla," the Duke said firmly.

"Well, if she goes on like this, Your Grace, she'll not be marrying anyone!" Hannah said. "I only hope as Your Grace knows what you're doing."

She bobbed the Duke a quick curtsey and, without waiting for him to say any more, went from the Library, wondering as she walked upstairs whether she should have said more, or perhaps less.

But something had to be done, although Hannah found it difficult to decide what it should be.

She went into the Sitting-Room next to Cyrilla's bedroom and found her, as she had expected, sitting at the window, staring out at the sunshine outside.

When Hannah came into the room she quickly picked up the book which lay on her lap, but the maid knew it was only pretence and she had not turned over a single page since Hannah had left her to go down-stairs.

"Your father's alone in the Library. Why don't you join him?"

"I will do so if you think he wants me," Cyrilla replied.

She rose, putting down her unread book as she did so.

It was her very submissiveness these days which made Hannah worry about her more than she would have done otherwise.

It was as if Cyrilla had no spirit, no feelings to express, because she was only partially alive. Almost like a puppet, she moved to the strings of those who pulled her, without using her own will, and having no interest in anything she did.

"It's that dratted man!" Hannah murmured under her breath as Cyrilla left the room.

* * *

The "dratted man," as Hannah called him, was at that moment riding along the dusty road which bordered the Duke's Park.

Where the stone wall was low he could look over it and through the trees to where the Castle loomed large and impressive in the sunshine.

It seemed at times to have an invulnerability that the Marquis found awe-inspiring.

It was as if it challenged him, and he was half-afraid that he could not win against such an insurmountable object.

No-one in London would have believed that the Marquis of Fane, with his comfortable houses and great possessions, would be living as he was now, in the discomfort of a small village Inn two miles from Holm Castle.

He had not been so foolish as to accommodate himself at the local Inn, which stood on the green just outside the Castle gates.

Yet there was quite a lot of speculation about him amongst the old men who sat outside the Crown and Anchor with their mugs of ale when he rode past them very early in the mornings and at several other times during the day.

What they did not know, because the Marquis was extremely careful, was that, hidden in the copses that were to be found all over the Park, he would watch Cyrilla riding with her father.

Although he could see her, he knew he dare not approach her. But it was better than being alone with only his thoughts of her.

The Inn in which he stayed was small and clean but extremely primitive.

The Marquis did not seem to notice the hardness of his bed or the difficulties of obtaining enough warm water to wash, or that the food he ate was, in his servants' opinion, hardly fit to serve to the pigs.

It was in fact his servants who suffered most, as they were acutely conscious of every discomfort and loathed staying in a small village with no entertainments or attractions when they might have been at Fane House.

The Marquis, however, was completely oblivious to everything but his need to see Cyrilla.

He thought that in her new riding-habit with its gauze veil floating behind her high-crowned hat, she looked so lovely and at the same time so insubstantial that it was understandable that her father kept them apart.

And yet, he told himself, somehow, in some way which he could not yet imagine, he had to make the Duke relent, had to force him to agree to their marriage.

So far, after a week of thought, he had come up with no solution to the puzzle and no ideas for the future.

He hoped every morning, while he waited for Cyrilla to appear in the Park, that she would be alone and the Duke would not be with her.

He dared not approach her when her father was there, for he knew it would be worse than useless and anything he might say would be ineffective and overruled by the Duke's authority.

The one chance he had of persuading her to agree that they must do something about their love would be if she was riding only with a groom or perhaps, which was improbable, alone.

But the days went by and always the Duke rode beside her. In the afternoons they would go driving and the Marquis would watch them, following unobserved at a discreet distance between the trees.

He thought that Cyrilla, in a fashionable bonnet with the ribbons tied under her chin, looked so lovely that even though he could not see her clearly his lips ached to kiss her, and he knew that he would give up his hope of Heaven to hold her once again in his arms.

Chapter Seven

"I spoke to you, Cyrilla!"

"I . . . I am . . . sorry . . . Papa."

Cyrilla spoke as if her mind had come back from a far distance, and the Duke, well aware of whom she had been thinking, felt his lips tighten before he managed to say in a pleasant manner:

"I was suggesting to you that this afternoon we should drive the new pair of bays that I bought for Edmund on his return."

"A new pair, Papa?"

"Yes. They were sold locally, and as I realised they were outstanding, although still not completely trained, I got them at a reasonable price."

"I am sure Edmund will be thrilled!"

"Go and put on your bonnet, and I will tell Burton to have the Phaeton brought round immediately."

Cyrilla rose obediently and gave her father a small smile before she walked towards the door.

He watched her leave the room, realising, as she did so, how thin she had grown and that Hannah was right in saying that she appeared to be wasting away.

He asked himself what he could do about it, and could find no answer to the question.

The Duke's Phaeton was very different from those owned by the Marquis and the Prince of Wales. They were High-Perch Phaetons, which were difficult to drive but which could travel at an amazingly fast rate, and they were, because they were so high, inclined to be dangerous.

However, painted in the Holm colours, his Phaeton, drawn by two perfectly matched bays, was very presentable, and the Duke picked up the reins as he said to the grooms:

"We are only going a short distance so shall not want you with us."

The grooms touched the brims of their hats and the Duke drove off.

He was an excellent driver, as Cyrilla remembered from the past, and she knew how much he would enjoy training the new horses for Edmund.

Because she was aware that it would please him, she said:

"I am counting the days until I shall see Edmund again, and now I know I shall be able to keep up with him when we are riding together!"

"I remember you used to complain because you were left behind on your pony," the Duke remarked.

"It was very humiliating that Edmund's mount was always bigger and faster than mine."

"Now that you are in practice again, you ride very well."

"I think both Edmund and I have taken after you, Papa," Cyrilla said, and realised that her father was pleased at the compliment.

They proceeded through the Park, then turned right, round a wood.

"Where are we going?" Cyrilla asked.

"I am not only trying out the horses," the Duke said, "but I want to call and see Jackson about some new buildings."

He paused to ask:

"Do you remember Jackson? He is the farmer who lives down at Dingle Bottom. Being lower than the rest of the countryside, it is a difficult place to farm."

"Of course I remember," Cyrilla replied.

They drove on, and now the road began to descend sharply towards Dingle Bottom, where the land was often water-logged in the winter and inclined to be swampy all the year round.

It was, however, an extremely pretty drive, with low hedges on either side of the road and a view of the Duke's Estate beyond, undulating away into the distance.

The Duke was pulling at the reins to make the horses proceed a little more slowly when suddenly over the hedge to the left of them jumped a stag.

It ran right in front of the bays, startling them in a manner which made one of them rear up and the other shy, catching a rein, as it did so, under the centre shaft.

For a moment the Phaeton rocked, then the two horses were galloping in a head-long manner out of control down the steep incline towards Dingle Bottom.

The Duke, pulling at the reins with all his strength, realised he was having little effect on their wild flight, and he knew that the road turned sharply at the bottom of the hill where it passed over a stone bridge.

Desperately he thought that unless he could free the rein caught under the shaft and check the other horse's mad dash, that was where they would crash.

But there was little time to think. He did wonder frantically whether he should tell Cyrilla to jump, then knew that to do so might prove even more disastrous than the crash would be.

It was only a question of seconds now; the bridge was ahead of them and there was nothing he could do. Exercising all his strength, he still was having no noticeable effect on the bays.

Then suddenly, from out of nowhere it seemed to the Duke, a man appeared on the road below them and, dismounting from his own horse, ran into the middle of the road to wait.

For a moment the Duke thought he must be mad.

Then as they reached him, with his arms outstretched he seized the bridles of both horses, holding them with an iron-like grip that forced them to check their speed, and the Duke realised that they had been saved.

He tightened his pull on the reins even more than he had done before, straining every nerve in his body, as he knew the man at the horses' heads was doing.

Slowly, within a few feet of the narrow bridge, the Phaeton was brought almost to a standstill.

It was then that the off-side bay reared up and his front hoof struck the side of the head of the man who was holding him.

He did not relinquish his grip, but his feet slipped, and as the horses went forward a few more paces, they dragged him with them.

The Duke heard Cyrilla scream, and a moment later she had sprung onto the road as the horses passed over the body of the man who had brought them to a standstill, and who now lay beneath the Phaeton.

The Duke could not leave his still-frightened animals, but he knew without turning his head that Cyrilla was kneeling on the ground beside the Marquis's prostrate body.

She was kissing his face frantically as the tears ran down hers.

* * *

"You'll need a great number of new suits, M'Lord."

"I am aware of that," the Marquis replied, staring at himself in the mirror.

It seemed incredible that he should have lost so much weight, and although his champagne-coloured pantaloons, being of the knitted material favoured by the Prince of Wales, were as tight as fashion decreed, his coat was undoubtedly unfashionably loose at the shoulders.

"Most gentlemen, M'Lord," his valet was saying, "put on weight when they've been laid up as Your Lordship 'as been, but then we don't expect you to be like anyone else!"

There was a pride in the valet's voice which the Marquis would have found amusing if he had been listening.

Instead, he was wondering if, now that the Doctor had allowed him to get back on his feet, the Duke would order him to leave the Castle.

He had not seen his host, an obviously reluctant one, since he had been carried back to the Castle.

First the local Doctor, and then Sir William Knifton, who had been fetched from London, had found that the Marquis had two ribs fractured, and was bruised in a manner which was not only extremely painful but made him look, he said disgustedly, like a "piebald pony."

But for a week he was in no condition to be critical about himself.

The first bay had struck him on the side of his head and he had been trampled by the other horse when he fell beneath the Phaeton.

When he had first returned to consciousness he could remember very little of what had happened. Then gradually he recalled how from his hiding-place in the woods he had watched Cyrilla driving with her father.

He had ridden along in the shelter of the trees, thinking how beautiful she looked and wondering, as he had done a thousand times before, how he could ever see her alone.

Vaguely he had noticed that the horses, a well-matched pair, were hard to handle, and it was only when they began to descend the sharp incline that he was aware that there might be any trouble.

He thought in fact that the Duke was going rather fast when he saw the stag jump in front of the horses, and instinctively he spurred his own mount forward.

It all happened in what in retrospect seemed a split second. He knew immediately what he must do if he was to save Cyrilla and was well aware of the danger of it.

But he knew too that nothing mattered except

that she should not be involved in a crash which was inevitable unless the horses could be brought under control.

"I understand," Sir William Knifton had said with a smile during his third visit to Holm Castle to see his distinguished patient, "that you have been playing the hero! You have a lot of decorations to show for it!"

"I can assure you they are damned painful," the Marquis replied.

"You are fortunate that things are not worse," Sir William said. "You might have broken an arm or a leg, or both."

"How soon can I get up?" the Marquis asked.

It had taken a great deal of persuasion on Sir William's part to make him realise that his ribs must heal.

However, because he knew how strong the Marquis was and how athletic, he told Fane's valet, who was as good a Nurse as any he could provide, that the Marquis's recovery would be a good deal quicker than might have been expected from any ordinary man who had been knocked about in such a manner.

"Keep him quiet for as long as you can," Sir William said to the valet before he left. "And because he hates to feel weak and consequently helpless, see that he has as much massage on his legs as he can stand, but do not dare touch his chest."

"I understand, Sir," Davis said.

He was a strong, wiry little man who had been with the Marquis for many years and was in his own way devoted to him.

In fact it was Davis who made the Marquis obey Sir William's orders, although he swore frequently that he would not be bullied.

Now at last he was on his feet and in fact feeling a great deal better than he had expected.

"I am going downstairs," he said aloud. "I am going to get some air, whatever you may say. I am sick to death of this room and everything in it!"

That was not entirely true, the Marquis knew as he said it.

By his bed and on the table near the window were two objects to which his eyes turned not once but practically every moment of the day.

They were two vases of lilies.

Lilies were the first thing he had seen when he had regained consciousness, and he had known who had sent them and that they were a message which told him that even though she might not see him, Cyrilla loved him.

He would lie in bed, and often the pain he was suffering, which at times was acute, would be forgotten when he saw her face in every lily and knew that the petals had the softness of her skin.

The lilies were the only communication he had with the inhabitants of the Castle where he was an involuntary guest.

The Duke did not come to see him and he knew Cyrilla would not be permitted to do so, and he was waited on only by his own valet.

Mr. Ashworth came down twice from London, but the Marquis was obviously so uninterested in anything he had to tell him that after he left he thought his visits were pointless.

He therefore told Davis that if the Marquis asked for him he would return, but otherwise he would wait until he was sent for.

"His Lordship's got things on his mind," Davis said, "besides what he calls 'the devil's own' pains in his body."

Mr. Ashworth was aware of what was on the Marquis's mind, but he drew no conclusions as to why he was at the Castle, until after he had seen Cyrilla.

He recognised her immediately from the portrait which stood in the Marquis's room, and on his return to London he paid off the Bow Street Runners. knowing that their services were no longer required.

"Well, I am ready," the Marquis said.

As he spoke, he took a last look at the crisp white freshness of his cravat, skilfully tied by Davis in a manner which always evoked the envy, hatred, and malice of the Dandies of St. James's.

There was a knock on the door. Davis opened it, spoke to someone outside, and came back to say:

"His Grace would be obliged, M'Lord, if you'd go to the Orangery."

The Marquis gave a sigh.

He had hoped that the Duke would have allowed him a little time to find his legs and have some fresh air before the inevitable interview which he could not help dreading.

He supposed, however, that he might as well get it over, and he wondered how he could send a message to Cyrilla that he must see her before the Duke threw him out of the Castle.

In fact, he told himself, he was damned if he would leave the Castle without doing so, without telling her how much he loved her and how hard he was trying to find a solution for their future.

All these past weeks he had lain in bed thinking of what he could say to make the Duke change his mind and give his consent to their marriage.

He thought it unlikely that his action in saving his life as well as Cyrilla's would influence a man who both despised and hated him and had done so for years, even before his daughter was involved.

The Duke was like all those who disapproved of the "Carlton House Set" and gave their loyalty and their unswerving allegiance to the King, mad though he might be.

The Marquis had thought about the whole situation for so long that he felt as if there was no aspect of it that he had not examined and pondered over until, by the process of elimination, he had almost lost hope of ever finding happiness for himself and Cyrilla.

Then as he walked towards the doors, he stopped for a moment to look at the vase of lilies on the table by the window.

The sunshine illuminated them with a light which gave the blooms a faint touch of gold and he thought of the radiance which always seemed to halo Cyrilla's head as it had in the Lochner painting.

He knew that without his own little "Virgin of the Lilies" life was bleak and desolate to the point where he wished that when the horses had trampled him underfoot they had killed him.

"How can I go on without her?" he asked himself, knowing that it would be impossible.

But how could he ever make the Duke understand that that was the truth?

He had changed in so many ways since he had known her, because his love for her had brought him a new understanding of people, besides making him capable of feeling emotions he had not known existed.

He looked back at his behaviour over the past years and felt shocked himself.

He saw how unfeeling and insensitive he had often been, and he admitted his selfishness and his egotism.

Loving Cyrilla had made him suffer in a manner that he had never conceived possible. He knew that in the future, if nothing else he would be more sympathetic and understanding of the sufferings of others.

"Now, be careful, Your Lordship, and don't do too much," Davis was saying. "I'll be waiting for you to come up and pop back into bed before dinner. Whatever Your Lordship may think now, you'll be glad enough later to lie back and take it easy."

It struck the Marquis that he might not be coming back to bed but instead would be driving away, if the Duke would no longer allow him to remain in the Castle.

But there was no point in saying so to Davis, and instead he merely put his hand on his valet's shoulder as he passed him, expressing without words his gratitude for all that the little man had done for him.

Davis understood, and his eyes as he followed his

Master to the top of the staircase were like those of a faithful spaniel.

The Marquis descended the stairs slowly and rather carefully, holding on to the bannister.

It was not hard to walk, since the massage that David had given his legs every day had kept the muscles strong as they had been before the accident.

But he was taking no risks. When he reached the Hall he asked one of the footmen on duty:

"Will you show me the way to the Orangery?"

"Yes, M'Lord."

The young man was eager to be of service to the man whom he had always admired for his sportsmanship and his success on the race-course.

And he was even more so when, although the Marquis was not aware of it, his action in saving the Duke and Cyrilla from what might have been a fatal accident had lost nothing in the telling.

In fact, the old yokels who sat outside the village Inns had been drinking his health in their mugs of ale.

" 'E be a real sportsman, tha's wot 'e be!" they said to one another, and downed another pint on the strength of it.

The Marquis proceeded along the corridor which led to the Orangery, which had been built on the south side of the Castle.

He thought it a strange place to have the serious conversation he was expecting with his host.

But he had learnt from Davis that the Duke was interested in growing rare plants, especially orchids.

He wondered if this was where Cyrilla had picked her lilies and if he would be able to thank her for the message they had brought him, which had cheered him even when he was most depressed.

Lilies as white, pure, and beautiful as she was; lilies that had been continuously a part of his thoughts of her ever since he had first seen her lovely face looking at him from the Lochner painting.

'I fell in love at first sight!' the Marquis thought.

The love he had known then had grown and grown until now it filled his whole world and it was impossible to think of anything except Cyrilla and his need of her.

He reached the Orangery, the footman opened the door, and the Marquis passed into the soft, warm, fragrant atmosphere.

There were rare orchids of every hue, exotic shrubs from foreign countries growing high against the roof, and azaleas from the foothills of the Himalayas.

Immediately in front of him there was a fountain iridescent in the sunshine which came through the long oval windows, the water from it falling with a musical sound into an exquisitely carved stone basin.

The Marquis looked round, expecting to see the Duke; then from behind the fountain, almost as if she emerged through the iridescent water itself, came Cyrilla!

The Marquis was very still. For a moment he could hardly believe that he was seeing her again after so long.

And yet she was there, as lovely as the lilies with which he had been comparing her a few minutes ago in his bedroom.

She walked very slowly towards him. Then when they were only a few feet from each other she said in a low voice:

"You ... are up! I did not ... realise you were ... well enough."

"I am well," the Marquis answered.

Their lips were saying one thing but their eyes, held by each other's, were saying something very different.

Then in a voice he barely recognised Cyrilla said:

"I have been so frightened ... so worried ... they said you would be ... all right ... but I found it ... hard to believe."

"But, as you see, I am."

"How could you have been so . . . brave? So incredibly . . . wonderfully . . . brave?" Cyrilla asked. "I
thought, before you . . . saved us, that I would . . . die
and never . . . see you again."

There was so much pain in her voice that instinctively the Marquis put out his hands towards her.

She took them in hers, saying:

"You . . . must . . . sit down . . . you must rest. I am
sure you are not well enough to . . . stand."

"I can do anything as long as I can see you!" the
Marquis answered.

He felt her drawing him a little to one side and
found that there was a marble seat covered with silk
cushions.

They sat down, their eyes still held by each
other's, and the Marquis thought, as he had so often
before, that it was impossible that anyone could be
so beautiful.

Yet at the same time he realised that Cyrilla was
thinner and there was something more spiritual about
her face than there had been before.

In fact, her eyes seemed unnaturally large, and
he knew it was not only because like him she had lost
a great deal of weight but because of the pain she
had suffered.

"You have not been ill, my darling?" he asked.

Cyrilla shook her head.

"N-no . . . only . . . worried about you."

"I have thought about you," he said. "I was so
afraid I would not see you. Only the lilies you sent me
gave me hope."

"I thought that you would . . . understand that I
could not . . . write to you or . . . see you."

"I understood," he said gently. "But what are
we to do, my precious?"

Cyrilla was still holding both his hands in hers
and now he felt her fingers trembling.

"What has your father said?" he asked quickly.

"Nothing! That is what makes it so difficult,"

Cyrilla replied. "I thought perhaps he would . . . talk to me after you had saved us both . . . but he did not do so . . . and I was afraid to make things worse."

"I understand," the Marquis said. "I will talk to him. In fact I was expecting to be doing so at this moment."

"He sent for you to come here?"

"Yes."

"How . . . strange!"

"Why?"

"Because he told . . . me to come to the . . . Orangery."

She looked at the Marquis and gave a little cry.

"He . . . meant us to . . . meet!"

"Perhaps he intended we should say good-bye," the Marquis said slowly. "It would, in the circumstances, be a kindness."

"G-good-bye? How can we . . . say good-bye to . . . each other?"

"That is what I am asking myself," the Marquis replied. "Oh, my lovely one, I have so much to tell you, so much to explain."

She took one of her hands from his and put two fingers on his lips to stop him speaking.

"There is . . . no need," she said. "I have thought it over . . . and I understand so many things I had not . . . understood before."

"What do you understand?" the Marquis asked gently.

"I . . . I may be . . . wrong," Cyrilla said a little hesitatingly, "but I feel that because you . . . wanted us to be alone . . . as I wanted it too . . . it simply did not occur to you that we . . . should get . . . married."

The Marquis looked at her as he said:

"How can you be so perfect, so wonderful, as to understand as no other woman could understand! That was the truth, my darling, the real truth. But I thought I could never make you believe it."

He paused for a moment before he went on:

"When I realised I had hurt you, when I knew what a fool I had been to lose you, I cursed myself over and over again for my stupidity."

"I too was ... foolish not to ... understand," Cyrilla said, "but it had been so ... horrible in many ways, knowing what Mama ... suffered because she ran away with Frans Wyntack. She loved him ... she loved him desperately ... but I thought that what she had ... endured would ... spoil our love."

"It would have done that," the Marquis said, "but if you had only told me, explained to me—"

"I know," Cyrilla interrupted. "I have thought about it a great deal ... and I did not understand ... then, as I do now, that love is greater than ... anything else ... greater and more important even than ... being married."

She drew in her breath before she said:

"If ... if you still want me ... and if Papa will not allow us to ... get married ... I will ... come away with you."

The Marquis's fingers tightened on hers.

"Do you think I could allow you to do that?" he asked. "I want you as my wife. I want you with me always, by day and by night, from now until eternity."

His voice was deep and intense with the emotions she had aroused in him. Then he added:

"But I worship you for what you have just suggested."

"If you will ... not take me ... away ... and Papa will not let us ... m-marry," Cyrilla said in a frightened voice, "what will happen to us?"

"This is a question I have asked myself a million times," the Marquis answered.

"I have ... prayed and prayed that somehow a miracle would happen and ... everything would be all right," Cyrilla whispered, "but ... sometimes I feel that no-one ... not even Mama ... hears my prayers."

"Your mother would understand what we are feeling."

"I know that," Cyrilla answered, "and perhaps

she would think I was being . . . foolish not to . . . come to you as you . . . wanted me to do, so that we could have been . . . together in that dear little house with the . . . garden."

"You were right at the time," the Marquis said. "You were absolutely right. I loved you, Cyrilla, but not in the way I do now, and because I worship you, my little 'Virgin of the Lilies,' with my whole heart and soul, I will not spoil or hurt you in any way."

"It would never . . . hurt me to be . . . with you."

"It would!" the Marquis said simply. "Only what is good and perfect is right where you are concerned. That is why, my darling, unless your father allows us to be married, I shall have to go away."

Cyrilla gave a little cry.

"I cannot lose you . . . I cannot! If you leave me . . . then I shall *die!*"

She only whispered the word and yet it seemed to ring out, and the Marquis looked at her and the pain in both their eyes seemed to link them in a manner in which they had never been linked before.

It was as if their lives merged one with the other and they were joined so that even death could not divide them.

Then as they looked despairingly into each other's souls, they heard the door of the Orangery open and footsteps coming towards them.

Neither the Marquis nor Cyrilla turned their heads. They were both aware who approached, and it seemed to the Marquis in that moment as if he stood on the edge of a cliff. Beneath him was a yawning gulf which led to destruction and above was the blue of the sky and the sunshine.

Without meaning to, his hand crushed Cyrilla's fingers until they were bloodless; then with a super-human effort he took his eyes from her and looked towards the Duke.

He stood beside them, looking very authoritative, with an expression on his face, the Marquis thought at a quick glance, that was stern.

He would have risen to his feet but the Duke put out his hand to prevent him.

"Do not rise, Fane," he said. "I imagine you will need to save your strength as this is the first time you have come downstairs."

"I can only thank you for your hospitality, Your Grace," the Marquis said formally.

As he spoke, it sounded as if his voice came from a long way away and was not really his own.

Because Cyrilla was near him, because of all they had been saying to each other, he found it hard to make his brain work at all, while to think clearly was almost impossible.

"I have been receiving good reports of your progress," the Duke said.

The Marquis drew in his breath.

"Perhaps, Your Grace, when it is convenient, I could talk to you privately."

As he spoke, the Marquis realised that the Duke was not looking at him but at Cyrilla.

Her face, which was very pale, was raised towards her father and her eyes had a look of pleading in them.

She made no effort to relinquish the Marquis's hand, in fact she was holding on to him as if she thought that at any moment they would be separated, perhaps forever.

It seemed to the Marquis as if a very long time elapsed; it might have been the passing of a second or a century before the Duke said to Cyrilla:

"I suggest, my dear, that in perhaps ten minutes' time you bring our guest into the Blue Salon. We will have tea there, and afterwards, if he is not too tired, we will make plans."

"Plans . . . Papa?"

Cyrilla's voice was barely above a whisper.

The Duke smiled.

"A wedding, whether it is large or small, always requires a great deal of planning, and we must try to choose a day when the gardens are looking their best."

The Duke walked away and they heard the door of the Orangery close behind him.

For a moment neither the Marquis nor Cyrilla was capable of moving. Then in a voice which was almost inaudible Cyrilla asked:

"Did you ... hear what he ... said ... or did I ... imagine it?"

The Marquis made a sound that was half-triumph and half-laughter.

"You heard, and I heard it too! Oh, my darling, my sweet! We have won! Do you realise? We have won and we need no longer be afraid!"

He pulled her towards him as he spoke, and his arms were round her, holding her close against him, his lips on her hair.

"We have won, my darling. We can be married and you can be mine. I shall no longer have to go on searching for my little 'Virgin of the Lilies.'"

Cyrilla's face was hidden in his shoulder and after a moment he said in a different tone:

"You are crying! My precious darling, do not cry!"

"I cannot ... believe it is ... true! I cannot ... believe that Papa really ... means it!" Cyrilla replied. "I am ... crying because I am ... so happy."

The Marquis had the uncomfortable feeling that he might cry too.

He knew it was weakness; and he knew too that it was an unutterable, incredible relief to know that Cyrilla would now be his.

Then with a touch of his old masterfulness he put his fingers under Cyrilla's chin and turned her face up to his.

"Everything has changed," he said softly, "and now there will be no more tears, no more unhappiness."

He looked down at her and there was a radiance in her eyes even while the tears were still on her cheeks and on her eye-lashes.

"I love you," he said. "I will make you happy and after this you will never cry again!"

"It is . . . true . . . it is . . . really true?"

"It is true!"

Then his lips were on hers.

As he kissed her, Cyrilla knew the wonder and glory she had known before, and yet there was a new dedication in the Marquis's kiss, and he felt that he was as overwhelmed with gratitude as she was.

This was the miracle she had prayed for; this was the moment when the darkness disappeared and they were swept away together into the light, the radiant light that came from God.

"I love . . . you! I love . . . you!" she cried.

The Marquis, holding her closer still, said quietly:

"It was love that made us find each other and has brought us through all our difficulties until we are together as we were always meant to be."

"It is so . . . perfect . . . so wonderful!" Cyrilla said. "Now I know something . . . which I shall never forget."

"What is that, my lovely one?" he asked.

"However much one tries, when love is real, the love that comes from God, no-one can deny it."

"It is something we both tried to do," the Marquis answered, "but it proved impossible not only for us but also for your father not to acknowledge it."

"We must thank him," Cyrilla said. "Just as we will thank . . . God because He has . . . given us the gift that is . . . part of Himself."

"That is exactly what it is," the Marquis agreed, "and you, my darling, are a child of God: good, pure, and perfect in every way, and I need you to help me."

Cyrilla gave a little smile that he thought was the most lovely thing he had ever seen.

"I want to help you," she said, "but not to alter you, because I love you just as you are. You are everything I always thought a man should be . . . kind, gentle, and very, very brave. How could I be so lucky as to find someone like . . . you?"

"It was not luck, it was fate," the Marquis said

firmly, "the fate which has been manipulating us since the very beginning."

As he spoke, he thought how true that was.

It was fate that he had made Frans Wyntack paint a fake of the Lochner; fate that had taken it to the Prince of Wales; fate that had made him paint Cyrilla again when he faked the Van Dyck.

Apart from even that long chain of strange co-incidences which could have been directed only by some force beyond themselves, it was fate that had brought him to the Castle when he had almost despaired of ever finding Cyrilla again.

A shower of rain, an accident, and damage to his wheel, and there was Cyrilla where he had least expected to find her!

The Marquis realised that he had been silent for some seconds and Cyrilla was looking at him enquiringly.

"Are you thinking about fate?" she asked.

"I suppose really I was thinking of you," the Marquis said. "I find it impossible to think of anything else."

"As I thought of you," she answered. "How could I have thought of anyone else when you were so near me? Yet I dared not . . . go to you. Sometimes I would . . . listen outside your door, hoping I would . . . hear your . . . voice."

"That is something you will never do in the future," the Marquis said. "You will be inside the door, close against my heart, and never—and this is a vow—I will never, never lose you."

She smiled at him and he thought it would be impossible for a woman to look so lovely and still be human and part of this world.

"I adore you!" he said now with a note of passion in his voice that had not been there before. "How soon can we be married?"

"The . . . garden is looking lovely . . . now!"

"Let us go and see your father," the Marquis said, "and please, my precious, impress upon him that if we are not allowed to marry very, very quickly, we will both waste away and there will be no wedding but only two ghosts to haunt the future generations at the Castle."

"That is ... something which will ... never happen."

Cyrilla rose to her feet as she spoke, and the Marquis got to his.

Then as they looked at each other, everything went from their minds and she was in his arms, and he was kissing her passionately, fiercely, and insistently, and yet she was not afraid.

This was love, divine and yet very human.

Cyrilla could feel the fire on the Marquis's lips and she knew that he was igniting a fire within her too.

She wanted him to kiss her and go on kissing her and for them to be closer and still closer to each other.

She did not quite understand what she felt, she knew only that it was very wonderful and it was love —the love from which they could never escape and which neither of them could deny.

ABOUT THE AUTHOR

BARBARA CARTLAND, the world's most famous romantic novelist, who is also an historian, playwright, lecturer, political speaker and television personality, has now written over 200 books.

She has also had many historical works published and has written four autobiographies as well as the biographies of her mother and that of her brother Ronald Cartland, who was the first Member of Parliament to be killed in the last war. This book has a preface by Sir Winston Churchill.

Barbara Cartland has sold 100 million books over the world, more than half of these in the U.S.A. She broke the world record in 1975 by writing twenty books, and her own record in 1976 with twenty-one. In addition, her album of love songs has just been published, sung with the Royal Philharmonic Orchestra.

In private life, Barbara Cartland, who is a Dame of the Order of St. John of Jerusalem, has fought for better conditions and salaries for Midwives and Nurses. As President of the Royal College of Midwives (Hertfordshire Branch), she has been invested with the first Badge of Office ever given in Great Britain which was subscribed to by the Midwives themselves. She has also championed the cause for old people and founded the first Romany Gypsy Camp in the world.

Barbara Cartland is deeply interested in Vitamin Therapy and is President of the British National Association for Health.

Barbara Cartland

The world's bestselling author of romantic fiction.
Her stories are always captivating tales of intrigue,
adventure and love.

☐	12841	THE DUKE AND THE PREACHER'S DAUGHTER	$1.50
☐	12569	THE GHOST WHO FELL IN LOVE	$1.50
☐	12572	THE DRUMS OF LOVE	$1.50
☐	12576	ALONE IN PARIS	$1.50
☐	12638	THE PRINCE AND THE PEKINGESE	$1.50
☐	12637	A SERPENT OF SATAN	$1.50
☐	12273	THE TREASURE IS LOVE	$1.50
☐	12785	THE LIGHT OF THE MOON	$1.50
☐	12792	PRISONER OF LOVE	$1.50
☐	12281	FLOWERS FOR THE GOD OF LOVE	$1.50
☐	12654	LOVE IN THE DARK	$1.50
☐	13036	A NIGHTINGALE SANG	$1.50
☐	13035	LOVE CLIMBS IN	$1.50
☐	12962	THE DUCHESS DISAPPEARED	$1.50

Buy them at your local bookstore or use this handy coupon for ordering:

Barbara Cartland

The world's bestselling author of romantic fiction. Her stories are always captivating tales of intrigue, adventure and love.

☐	11410	THE NAKED BATTLE	$1.50
☐	11512	THE HELL-CAT AND THE KING	$1.50
☐	11537	NO ESCAPE FROM LOVE	$1.50
☐	11580	THE CASTLE MADE FOR LOVE	$1.50
☐	11579	THE SIGN OF LOVE	$1.50
☐	11595	THE SAINT AND THE SINNER	$1.50
☐	11649	A FUGITIVE FROM LOVE	$1.50
☐	11797	THE TWISTS AND TURNS OF LOVE	$1.50
☐	11801	THE PROBLEMS OF LOVE	$1.50
☐	11751	LOVE LEAVES AT MIDNIGHT	$1.50
☐	11882	MAGIC OR MIRAGE	$1.50
☐	11959	LORD RAVENSCAR'S REVENGE	$1.50
☐	11488	THE WILD, UNWILLING WIFE	$1.50
☐	11555	LOVE, LORDS, AND LADY-BIRDS	$1.50